HARLEQUIN®
Presents~

Great news! From this month onward,
Harlequin Presents® is offering you more!

Now, when you go to your local bookstore, you'll
find that you have *eight* Harlequin Presents® titles
to choose from—more of your favorite authors,
more of the stories you love.

To help you make your selection from our July
books, here are the fabulous titles that are available:
Prince of the Desert by Penny Jordan—hot desert
nights! *The Scorsolini Marriage Bargain* by
Lucy Monroe—the final part of an unforgettable
royal trilogy! *Naked in His Arms* by Sandra Marton—
the third Knight Brothers story and a sensationally
sensual read to boot! *The Secret Baby Revenge* by
Emma Darcy—a passionate Latin lover and a shocking
secret from his past! *At the Greek Tycoon's Bidding*
by Cathy Williams—an ordinary girl and the most
gorgeous Greek millionaire! *The Italian's Convenient
Wife* by Catherine Spencer—passion, tears and joy
as a marriage is announced! *The Jet-Set Seduction*
by Sandra Field—fasten your seat belt and prepare
to be whisked away to glamorous foreign locations!
Mistress on Demand by Maggie Cox—he's rich,
ruthless and really...irresistible!

Remember, in July, Harlequin Presents® promises
more reading pleasure. Enjoy!

Arabian Nights

by
Penny Jordan

Spent at the Sheikh's pleasure…

The Sheikh's Virgin Bride #2325
One Night with the Sheikh #2332
Possessed by the Sheikh #2457
Prince of the Desert #2547

Welcome back to the exotic land of Zuran,
a beautiful romantic place
where anything is possible.

Experience a night of passion
under a desert moon
in Harlequin Presents®

Penny Jordan

PRINCE OF THE DESERT

Arabian Nights

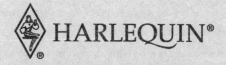

HARLEQUIN®

TORONTO • NEW YORK • LONDON
AMSTERDAM • PARIS • SYDNEY • HAMBURG
STOCKHOLM • ATHENS • TOKYO • MILAN • MADRID
PRAGUE • WARSAW • BUDAPEST • AUCKLAND

ISBN-13: 978-0-373-12547-0
ISBN-10:   0-373-12547-X

PRINCE OF THE DESERT

First North American Publication 2006.

Copyright © 2006 by Penny Jordan.

This edition published by arrangement with Harlequin Books S.A.

® and TM are trademarks of the publisher. Trademarks indicated with
® are registered in the United States Patent and Trademark Office, the
Canadian Trade Marks Office and in other countries.

www.eHarlequin.com

Printed in U.S.A.

All about the author...
Penny Jordan

PENNY JORDAN has been writing for more than twenty-five years and has an outstanding record: over 165 novels published, including the phenomenally successful *A Perfect Family, To Love, Honour and Betray, The Perfect Sinner* and *Power Play,* which hit the *Sunday Times* and *New York Times* bestseller lists. She says she hopes to go on writing until she has passed the 200 mark, and maybe even the 250 mark.

Although Penny was born in Preston, Lancashire, U.K., and spent her childhood there, as a teenager she moved to Cheshire, and has continued to live there. Following the death of her husband she moved to the small traditional Cheshire market town on which she based her CRIGHTONS books.

She lives with a large hairy German shepherd— Sheba—and an equally hairy Birman cat—Posh— both of whom assist her with her writing. Posh sits on the newspapers and magazines that Penny reads to provide her with ideas she can adapt for her fictional books and Sheba by demanding the long walks that help Penny to free up the mental creative process.

Penny is a member and supporter of both the Romantic Novelists' Association and the Romance Writers of America—two organizations dedicated to providing support for both published and yet-to-be-published authors.

CHAPTER ONE

GWYNNETH exhaled with exhaustion as she paid off the taxi driver and stood looking up at the building in front of her—the building that contained her father's apartment. No, not her father's apartment any more, she reminded herself bleakly, but her own. Her father was dead, and in his will he had left all his assets to her.

And his responsibilities? He might not have willed those to her, but she nonetheless felt morally obliged to make them her own. Her slender shoulders bowed slightly. The last few weeks had taken their toll on her. Her father's fatal heart attack had been shockingly unexpected. It might be true that they had never shared a traditional father and daughter relationship. How could they have? But that didn't mean she hadn't cared about him. He was—*had been*—her father, after all.

Yes, it was true that after her parents' divorce her father had virtually abandoned her into the unloving care of her mother and stepfather. It was true that he had been absent from her life for most of the time she had been growing up, whilst he pursued his own hedonistic lifestyle and travelled the world. And it was also true that his absence had only been punctuated by sporadic visits to the small private boarding school where she had been left and virtually brought up by its kindly elderly headmistress. But of the two of them it was her mother who had hurt her the most. When a person had wealth and power, that person could break the rules and then remake them. And her stepfather was both very wealthy *and* very powerful.

Unlike her father, whose main assets had been his charismatic personality and his persuasive tongue. A rueful smile curved her lips as she remembered how he had boasted to her that it was via that latter asset that he had acquired this apartment in the Persian Gulf Kingdom of Zuran.

'The block it's in is right in the middle of a new marina development. I'm telling you, Gwynneth, I could have sold it ten times—no, a hundred times over, for double what I paid for it,' he had told her excitedly.

Gwynneth hadn't known very much about the desert kingdom of Zuran then—but she did now. Which was why she was here.

She shivered a little in the almost disturbingly sensual warmth of the Arabian Gulf night. It wrapped round her like silken gauze, teasing her skin with its subtle caress, cloaking the intimacy of its effect on her with its darkness, like a mystery lover whose face was hidden from her, his touch all the more erotic for being unknown. A deep shudder gripped her body as she tried to pull down the defensive inner blinds she always used to block out such sensual thoughts. She had fought all her adult female life to separate herself from the dangers of the deep, dark core of sexuality she had inherited from her father, which she tried so hard to deny and ignore.

So *why*, knowing that, had she reacted so emotionally to his recent claim that she was devoid of sexuality, and thus deprived of the pleasure of enjoying that sexuality? That was what she wanted, what she had chosen for herself, and so his words should have brought her pleasure instead of making her searingly conscious of what she was missing.

It was the stress of the last few weeks that was weakening those defences, somehow allowing an unfamiliar hunger and need to well up so forcefully inside her, she assured herself wearily. It was gone midnight here in Zuran, even though it was still only early evening at home.

She lifted her hand to push the slightly 'boho' tangle of long red-gold curls back off her face as she closed the sometimes too eloquent green eyes that, even at twenty-six, she could still not always control, and which could so easily betray what she was feeling. Like her dark eyelashes and her creamy skin, they were her heritage from her Irish mother, just as the delicacy of her bone structure and her supple, slender figure had come down from her paternal grandmother—at least according to her father. He had certainly once been a very handsome man. Once…

The familiar pain-cum-anger-cum-anguish knotted the muscles of her stomach. Her eyes opened, shadowed by hurtful memories. As a child she had often wondered what exactly she had done to deserve parents who did not love her. As an adult she had learned to tell herself that it was their inability to love one another that was responsible for their inability to love her, the child they had accidentally produced but never wanted.

Her mother had remarried within a year of the divorce, departing for Australia with her new husband to make a new life for herself. Her father, freed from a marriage he'd claimed he had never wanted, had roamed the world drinking, gambling, and on rare occasions turning up in England to see her—invariably when he was stoned, broke or drunk, and sometimes all three. A member of the hippy generation, her father had still in middle age embraced drugs and drink and the 'free love' culture. Had done. But no longer did—no longer could. Despite his lifestyle she had still been shocked by his death. A heart attack, the hospital had informed her, his daughter and next of kin.

His daughter, but not his only child. How could a man who had abandoned one child because he hadn't wanted her have so carelessly fathered a second?

She had had no idea of what was to happen when he'd telephoned out of the blue and told her that he was in London and staying at one of its most exclusive hotels. She had gone straight from the City bank where she worked as an analyst to the hotel where, to her surprise, she had discovered he was staying in not merely a room but a suite. Then had come the discovery that he had not come to London on his own, but had brought with him his Filipina girlfriend, Teresa, and their baby son.

'Teresa looks so young,' Gwynneth had protested, unable to conceal her distaste at the thought of such a young and pretty girl with a man as life-worn and jaded as her father.

'She's twenty-two,' he had told her carelessly.

Four years younger than she was herself. Her expression had obviously given her away, because he had shrugged his shoulders and told her unashamedly, 'You can look like that all you want. So I enjoy sex. So what's wrong with that? I never thought any kid of mine would turn out to be a sexless prude. Sex is a natural, normal, adult human appetite that should be a source of pleasure, not hang-ups. You don't know what you're missing. If I were you—'

'I don't want to know,' she had answered him sharply. 'And you aren't me.'

She had always known the danger of her inherited sensuality—just as she had always fought to repress it. But now, without her father here to remind her of why she was so determined to flatline her own sexuality, disturbing weaknesses had begun to appear in what she had believed to be the impregnable wall of her immunity to physical desire.

She looked up at the building in front of her again, and double-checked to make sure she had the right address before exhaling in relief. She had half expected to find her father had been exaggerating when he'd boasted to her about the luxury apartment he owned in what he had described as the most exclusive apartment block in Zuran.

Now, though, she could see that the development was every bit as exclusive as he had claimed. She could see the gleaming white hulls of luxury yachts bobbing gently on the protected waters of the marina in the moonlight. In the distance, at the end of a curved breakwater, she could see what looked like an all-glass restaurant, floodlit from beneath. Immaculate gardens surrounded the apartment block, which was one of several all linked together by glass walkways and gardens to an elegant hotel, and all set on the same spit of land, with the marina on one side of it and a private beach on the other. A true millionaire's paradise. But her father had not been a millionaire. He had been a wheeler-dealer, a chancer. Sometimes making money but more often than not losing it.

She had been dubious at first when she had taken the deeds of the apartment to have them checked out, but she had been assured by the Zurani Embassy in London that they were genuine.

Unfortunately, though, as they had explained politely, for legal reasons, in order to re-register the apartment in her name she would either have to go out to Zuran itself or appoint someone within Zuran to act for her.

Since she had not been happy with the idea of handing over the documentation relating to her father's ownership of the apartment to someone else, she had decided that she would have to come out to Zuran herself.

Removing her father's pass key from her handbag, Gwynneth walked determinedly towards the entrance, half expecting to be stopped or at least challenged, but to her relief the glass doors opened as swiftly and silently as though she had commanded *Open Sesame*. Of course the pass key was the modern equivalent to those magical words.

A lift—also activated by the pass key—took her up to the penthouse suite floor. She had no idea how much the apartment was worth, but surely it had to be a reasonably large sum? She wanted to get it sold as quickly as she could. The pressure on her bank account was increasing every day. She earned a reasonable salary, but she had her mortgage to cover, and other outgoings. Her father's bank accounts had been virtually empty, which meant that she had had to pay for his funeral as well as his hotel bill. At least with her here in Zuran there would be more room in her small flat for Teresa and baby Anthony, whom she had felt honour-bound to do all she could to help. Her stomach churned with nausea.

One thing at a time, she reminded herself firmly. One thing at a time. She slid the pass key into the lock, and exhaled slowly in relief as the light flashed green.

Double doors opened from the hallway into a corridor. Immediately facing her was another pair of double doors.

When she opened them she found that they led into a huge living room, elegantly furnished with a mix of modern and reproduction antique furniture, including a low divan heaped with cushions and covered with richly coloured silk and damask fabrics.

Her father had told her that he had not as yet stayed in the apartment himself. He had bought it off plan, fully furnished and ready to move into, right down to the bedlinen and towels, all chosen by a top-flight interior designer. This room certainly had an immaculate 'show house' air about it—right down to the subtle scent of sandalwood. This was a room designed to embrace each one of the five senses.

Off the living room she found an immaculate galley kitchen, complete with a fridge that dispensed iced water, and a terraced balcony with table and chairs. But right now it wasn't either food or drink she craved so much as sleep.

She found the bedroom at the other end of the corridor, and pushed open the door. She came to an abrupt halt. Its decor was so sensually opulent that just looking at it made her skin prickle with sensory overload. It was decorated in a blend of creams and beiges dramatically highlighted with black, and with the lavish use of rich fabrics and gilt-framed mirrors.

She went back to the corridor and opened the remaining door. Maybe originally the room had been intended to be used as a bedroom, but right now it was furnished as a home office.

She had left her case in the hallway and she went back to get it. She frowned a little to see that the main door did not have any kind of security chain, and then shrugged mentally as she reassured herself that it was impossible to get into the building without a pass key.

It was almost one o'clock, and she had an appointment with the government agency dealing with the ownership of Zurani property by foreign nationals in the morning, she reminded herself. And she undressed and stepped into the shower of the marble *en suite* bathroom.

Fifteen minutes later she was in bed and fast asleep.

'Tariq.'

A warm smile illuminated the face of Zuran's ruler as he greeted one of his favourite relatives. He embraced him as his equal, ruler to ruler, for although in Zuran *he* was the Ruler, and Tariq one of his subjects, Tariq's own small kingdom— a remote hidden valley where the desert met the mountains— meant that he was also a prince in his own right. 'I hear that you hope to begin work soon on the excavation of the ancient city of your ancestors?'

Tariq smiled back. 'Once the heat of the summer is over, work will start.'

'And you would rather be there, scratching around in the sand, than here at my court?' The Ruler laughed as he studied the younger man.

Although they were both wearing traditional Arab dress, Tariq was clean-shaven where the Ruler was bearded, grey-eyed where the Ruler's eyes were a more traditional dark brown, and his skin was more sun-browned than naturally olive, betraying his dual heritage. However, the two men shared the same arrogantly hawkish profile and the same scimitar-like mouths, the same pride of bearing and aware-ness of who and what they were.

The Ruler reached out and placed his hand on the younger man's arm whilst Tariq maintained a diplomatic silence. He had fondness and a great respect for the Ruler, both as a monarch and as a friend.

When his late mother's marriage had ended, after her British husband—his father—had walked out on them, she had accepted an invitation from the Ruler's late father to make her home beneath his roof rather than live alone with her young son. Tariq had virtually grown up here at the palace, although along with many other young men from Zuran he had received his schooling in England and America.

'So,' the Ruler invited him, 'what progress is there with your investigations into this matter of the double selling of those properties that were made available for purchase by non-Zurani nationals?

Tariq waved away the dish of sweetmeats he was being offered, the scimitar-shaped mouth softening into an amused smile as his somewhat plump relative bit into one. The Ruler was known for his sweet tooth.

'The leader of the gang—Chad—is a South African, and I have now been allowed to meet him. He has intimated to me that he is already receiving the help of someone high up within the Zurani Government, who has been providing them with the documents they need to claim ownership of the properties. They are then illegally selling them on, at an inflated price, and not just to one buyer but to two, doubling their profit. By the time their victims discover that they do not own the properties they believe they have bought it is too late— their money has gone.

'Unfortunately at the moment the gang leader obviously doesn't trust me enough to give me the name of the Zurani official who is assisting him. Chad is too clever to put himself at risk—so much so, in fact, that he controls his criminal operation from a sea-going yacht. As you know, I have represented myself to the gang as someone whose services can be bought—a disaffected and profoundly greedy junior member of the Zurani Royal Family—in the hope that the promise of my potential influence will cause them to reveal the identity of their contact. But Chad is a very cautious and suspicious man. It is obviously not enough for him that I have accepted the bribe he has already offered me, in the form of one of the apartments they have now acquired with my assistance.'

'This, of course, is the apartment in which you are now living?'

'It seemed a good way to reinforce his belief in my greed. I've also claimed that I'm short of ready cash because the inheritance from my mother is being kept from me and controlled by you. Although to cover myself I have let it be known that this is not public knowledge.' Tariq shrugged. 'After all, we must assume that whoever it is who is helping them will know who I am, and of my family's wealth, so they have to believe in my grudge-bearing and acquisitive nature.'

'I sense that you are not entirely happy with the role you have been called upon to play,' the Ruler remarked sympathetically. 'But you are one of the few people in whom I have absolute trust, Tariq, and this is a very sensitive matter.'

'Indeed! So far all the victims we know about have stated that they bought their property via a supposed "official agent". Unfortunately,' he added dryly, 'since this agent dressed in traditional Arab dress, had a beard and wore very large sunglasses, none of them felt able to recognise and identify him. We must assume that he either was or is connected with the Zurani official who is helping the gang. That being the case, if what is happening becomes public knowledge in the international arena it will damage Zuran's reputation very badly.'

'That must not be allowed to happen. This man must be found and unmasked,' said the Ruler sternly, his expression softening as he added, 'I know that I can trust you to do whatever is necessary.'

Having dismissed his car and driver a safe distance away from the apartment, Tariq paused to breathe in the warm late-night air. It was on nights like this that the desert called to him so strongly that his desire to leave the city behind and satisfy his need to return to it became a hunger in his soul.

He thought with contempt of the corrupt gang of men he was currently involved with. Only last night their leader had promised him the services of one of the skimpily dressed prostitutes who were also on board the yacht, as a further reward for Tariq's support.

Of course he'd had to pretend to be flattered by the offer, even though in reality he had been utterly revolted by the sleaziness of both the gang and their leader's offer. He had declined to accept, using the excuse that he was afraid that it might get to the ears of his cousin the Ruler, who would then be even less inclined to allow him control of his inheritance.

Despite the fact that he had been celibate for the last eighteen months—since the termination of a discreet relationship he had shared with an elegant divorced Frenchwoman who, like him, had had no desire to commit herself to marriage—the sight of the skimpily clad young women with their surgically enhanced breasts and vacant eyes had not aroused him at all. How many other members of the gang had enjoyed their favours? Some of them? All of them? And more? Other men as well?

His mouth curled in contemptuous disgust as he recalled how the gang leader had offered slyly, 'Why don't I arrange to have one of them sent up to your apartment so that you can enjoy her in private?'

'Thank you, but no,' Tariq had responded, feigning regret.

He reached the apartment block, and, reaching for his pass key, inserted it into the lock and waited for the doors to open.

Once inside the apartment Tariq strode through to the bedroom without bothering to switch on the light or glance towards the bed, stripping off before going into the wetroom attached to the *en suite* bathroom and then standing beneath the fierce lash of the shower.

Gwynneth woke up abruptly. Her face was on fire whilst her body ached with a different kind of heat. Why was this happening to her *now*, after all these years? Why had physical desire chosen *now* to voice its protest at her denial of it?

Her father had laughed at her and accused her of being unable to understand sexual desire. But she did understand it. She understood it all too well, she admitted. She understood her own vulnerability to it—which was why she had forced herself to learn to control it, to repress and restrain it, out of fear that it would lead her to become like him. But now, suddenly, she couldn't control it. It pulsed hotly and urgently within her body, clamouring for release, shocking and confusing her.

Abruptly she sat up in the bed—at the exact moment that Tariq opened the door from the *en suite* bathroom.

Gwynneth stared in mute disbelief at the man standing in the doorway, framed by the light from the bathroom behind him. Like her, he was completely naked. Well, no, he was not actually like her at all, she thought feverishly. His skin was warmly tanned where hers was pale, his shoulders broad, his chest softly furred with silky dark hair, his belly flat. He was, she acknowledged, the most sexily physically perfect man she could ever have imagined. Tall, dark and handsome. Plus he had that edgy, dangerous male air that produced a female frisson of erotic fear within her—the kind of fear that was not fear at all, but rather an excitement that was morally shocking. One brief glance. That was all she needed to tell her that everything about him pushed all the right buttons for her. How on earth had she conjured him up? She blinked determinedly. This couldn't really be happening. He was an illusion, a figment of her imagination.

Only he was still there, and no amount of blinking seemed to be banishing him. Which meant… Which meant that he had to be real! Hurriedly Gwynneth looked away from him, her face starting to burn.

It was that over-acted fake look of confusion with which she turned her head and then let it droop on the pale stem of her neck that was responsible for the savage increase in his anger, Tariq decided as he demanded bitingly, 'How did you get in here?'

As if he needed to ask. He knew perfectly well what she was and who was responsible for her presence here in his apartment—and in his bed.

Striding towards her, he said curtly, 'No, don't bother answering me. I already know the answer—just as I know exactly what you are!' He gave her a look of icy disdain. No way was she staying here. He wanted her out of the apartment—and speedily, even if that meant he had to dress her himself.

Her naked man wasn't an illusion at all, or a figment of her imagination. He was very much real, and he had almost reached the bed, Gwynneth realised in panic, her trapped gaze skittering away from his chest.

She cried out in protest as his fingers tightened round her upper arm, instinctively trying to pull away from him as he virtually hauled her off the bed.

At least *these* breasts were real, Tariq couldn't help thinking, as he monitored the gentle bounce produced by her agitated movements and remembered the unmoving plastic look of the surgically enhanced breasts of the girls he had seen on the yacht and thought so repulsive. A woman's breasts surely should be soft and malleable, just big enough to fill a man's cupped hand, as this woman's breasts would surely do. He could almost imagine how they would feel, her skin warm, her nipples tightening against his touch, her breasts swelling with arousal just as his own body—

The shock of what he was experiencing exploded into savage disbelief. He couldn't possibly be aroused by her.

'What are you doing? Let go of me!' She couldn't just give in to him, Gwynneth told herself wildly as she pushed frantically against his chest with her free hand.

'Where are your clothes?'

Her clothes? His question bemused her, making her frown slightly.

Tariq could feel the silky length of her hair brushing his chest as she dipped her head and tried to raise her arms to conceal her naked breasts. Her skin looked milky pale against his own, the movement of her arms bringing the fingers he had wrapped around her arm into contact with the soft flesh of her breast. Her eyes were a deep jade, her lips the soft pink of the inside of a shell dredged up from the depths of the gulf. His gaze dropped from her mouth to her breasts, creamy pale flesh mounted with warm brown nipples that were swelling and hardening beneath the heat of his gaze.

Gwynneth could hear the sound of her own breathing, feel the heavy sensual pound of her own blood. Her gaze, no longer under her control, dropped boldly down his body to where she had been so determined not to look, and a small sound that she would not allow to be a soft moan of pleasure leaked from her lungs.

Tariq could feel the savage surge of his own anger racing through him, overturning everything in its way. Anger against the woman he was holding, anger against the men who had sent her to him, anger against so many things—but most of all anger against himself. He was simply not prepared to admit to the unwanted piercing stab of desire that was currently arcing through him. It was impossible for him to be aroused by a woman such as this, impossible for him to want her, impossible for him to touch her. But, impossible or not, all three of those things were happening.

CHAPTER TWO

THIS couldn't possibly be happening, Gwynneth decided breathlessly. She could not be standing here naked, body-to-body with this man who was a stranger to her but whom her body was welcoming with such rejoicing.

And yet when he turned her towards him she reached out and touched his face with her fingertips, slowly exploring its structure. His flesh felt warm against the hard contours of his bones, and something about the sheer male arrogance and power of him set off a quivering sensation of wanton excitement inside her. She could feel the heat of his grey-eyed gaze burning into her own skin, her breath catching in her throat as she looked at the thick clumped black lashes shielding his eyes from her. His hands were resting on her waist, almost spanning it. They slid down to her bottom, kneading her flesh, pressing her into his own body and its hard erection. She made a soft sound of pleasure, rubbing herself against him, reaching up to pull his head down towards her so that she could offer up her mouth for him to plunder. The kneading had become a rhythm he was slowly forcing on her own body, using pleasure to make her flesh accept and reciprocate the sensual beat of physical arousal. Now she knew why the sound of softly beaten drums could be so erotic, Gwynneth thought feverishly, as his mouth took hers and his tongue reinforced the rhythm he had set her body.

Now she was her father's daughter. Now she was obeying the call of her own blood. Now she was exposed to that need within herself she had always tried to deny. Now she was not denying it, though. She was embracing it, welcoming it, abandoning herself to it, physically powerless to resist the relentless drive of her own need, and emotionally too flooded with what she was feeling even to want to do so.

There was a pagan drive within her, a stream of subconscious need from the dawn of womanhood, imprinting itself relentlessly over every protective pattern she had ever tried to teach her body.

She *wanted* to feel like this, she recognised dizzily. She needed to experience what she was now experiencing; she needed to take the sweet juicy flesh of sexual arousal and taste every bit of it, savouring its taste and its texture on her fingers, her lips, her tongue, in her mouth, her belly, her deepest self. She wanted to linger over every delicious mouthful, to breathe in its scent, absorb its reality; she wanted to take her own sexuality and relish every second of experiencing its coming of age.

These thoughts flashed hypnotically through her mind, glinting like tiny shoals of brilliantly coloured fish, dizzying in their speed and beauty.

Chad had certainly known what he was about in choosing to send this woman to him, Tariq recognised as his self-control gave up the fight to force his body not to respond to the dangerous shimmering sensuality she exuded. It was almost as though it surrounded her in a multi-layered invisible aura that weakened and then trapped his treacherous senses, until nothing mattered more than satisfying his desire for her.

The increasingly charged sound of their breathing echoed erotically on the sandalwood-scented air. Their lips met, their tongues entwining, and Gwynneth's soft moans were echoed by Tariq's harsher sound of raw male need. Gwynneth kissed his throat, sliding her open mouth over his newly sweat-dampened flesh, tasting the little beads of arousal glistening against the smooth tanned flesh, savouring the fresh, erotically musky scent with which his body was telling her its need. The feel of his hands spread over her bottom, pressing her closer to him, made her sigh with liquid pleasure. His hands stroked upwards to her waist, and up again, whilst the hard thrust of his thigh parted her own. His hands cupped her breasts. She moaned in eager delight, her teeth nipping at the strong column of his throat, her fingers digging into the muscles of his back as her body arched in a torment of longing.

Tariq swung her up into his arms. The moonlight shining in through his bedroom windows highlighted her slender delicacy, silvering the thrust of her hipbones and her desire-swollen mound, whilst shadows deepened the dark allure of her tightly erect nipples.

He had reached the bed, but, too impatient to wait until he had placed her on it, Tariq laid her back against his bent leg, one arm supporting her whilst he looked down at her. He could see the contraction of her ribcage as she breathed, could see too the tiny shudders of arousal quivering over her as she looked up at him, wantonly offering herself up to his visual and physical possession.

How could she be feeling this intensity of physical excitement in lying here, knowing that she was offering her body up to this stranger as a source of erotic pleasure they could both share and enjoy? How could she have come to disassociate herself from her flesh, as though she and this man were co-conspirators, both intent on the same goal of sharing the feast of sensuality they had prepared?

Tariq reached out and slowly stroked his fingertips from the base of her throat down between her breasts, watching as her heart jumped and her breathing deepened, moving lower across the concave dip of her belly to stroke up to the swollen flesh and soft hair covering her pubic bone.

He leaned forward, his tongue flicking against the hollow of her throat as his fingers carefully parted the folded outer lips of her sex.

The flick of his tongue-tip and the stroke of his fingers seemed to create a taut cord of intensity that coiled her pleasure higher and tighter with every touch.

When he lowered her to the bed, without ceasing to caress her, she reached up for him, telling him urgently how good his touch felt, then shuddering when he cupped her breast with his free hand, savouring the erotic texture of her nipple and its response to his sensual stimulation.

Mindlessly Gwynneth reached out for him, her eyes widening and her gaze focusing hotly on him as she tried to enclose him within her grip and realised his potency.

When she exhaled, it was with an instinctive and deep-rooted female recognition of sensual pleasure at his size and strength. Somehow, she realised, her body, her senses, had a knowledge that she herself had never allowed them.

Deep within her female muscles flexed and female flesh heated, whilst a sound that was almost a voluptuous purr of anticipated pleasure vibrated in her throat.

The male flesh she was touching felt hot and slick, the movement of the skin she was rhythmically caressing unexpectedly erotic to her own senses. She moved demandingly on the bed, opening her legs and arching her back as Tariq's fingers stroked over her, experiencing a pleasure that turned her body liquid with aching need.

Had there ever been another woman like this one? Surely she was unique in her erotic offering of herself, in her sensual abandonment to her own pleasure? It took from him the role of being pleasured and demanded instead that he should make himself the provider of her pleasure. She was surely a queen amongst houris, demanding his subservience to her desire, Tariq acknowledged, and the intensity of his own physical desire burned away both his pride and his contempt.

Her tight, erect nipples demanded the worship of his gaze, his touch and his tongue-tip. But to draw one fully into his mouth and to pleasure it rhythmically as he suckled on its swollen heat would, he knew, be a pleasure too far for his self-control. However, the slender fingers sliding into his hair and commanding that he did just that could not be denied.

Gwynneth moaned and trembled convulsively as pleasure leapt fiercely inside her, her fingers tightening around the hard, hot shaft of male flesh that was moving within her grasp in quick urgent strokes, whilst knowing male fingers stroked and tugged the swollen flesh of her clitoris until she cried out aloud in a frenzy of arousal that took her higher and higher, so high that she felt she couldn't bear any more. But even as she cried out against what she was feeling her orgasm was overwhelming her. She heard the man call out, but his words meant nothing. Her body shuddered into its own completion.

It was the way she had abandoned herself so utterly to her

own fulfilment that had thrust him past the barriers he had imposed on himself and overwhelmed his self-control, Tariq decided grimly as he moved away from her to deal with the resolution of his own release.

Five minutes later, when he returned from the bathroom, she was fast asleep.

Tariq frowned as he looked down at her. Why hadn't she dressed and left? That was certainly what he would have preferred her to have done—wasn't it? She opened her eyes and looked up at him and smiled. And then she closed them again. By the time he had exhaled, very, very slowly, she had fallen asleep again.

Still frowning, he pulled the covers over her. At least that way her body was concealed and could no longer be the source of any kind of temptation to him. He should feel nothing but disgust for himself. He *did* feel disgust for himself, Tariq decided grimly. How could he have wanted a woman who sold herself to any man who could afford to buy her? What hitherto unknown to him part of himself had she managed to reach in order to arouse a desire in him strong enough to overwhelm his self-control?

The blending of East and West that was his heritage had given him the advantage of not having any desire to experience the wanton sexuality so freely exhibited by so many Western women. He had never, as other Arab men he knew did, felt any urge to provide himself with the services of a Western mistress, a woman with whom he could have sex without censure and whom he could dismiss from his life when he chose.

Zuran's exclusive hotels did not permit the kind of behaviour indulged in by young Westerners in other foreign resorts.

Topless sunbathing, any kind of intimacy with a man in public—these things were banned by law. But there were men, rich men, who brought with them to Zuran women who were quite plainly not their wives. And, as he was discovering, Zuran had now become a target for the kind of sordid, seedy lifestyle he deplored, for drugs and prostitution racketeers. He was under no illusions; it was common knowledge that the two went hand in hand.

But, even knowing all of that, he had still been unable to stop himself from reacting to the skilled sensuality of a woman he simply shouldn't have wanted to touch.

How many of the other men in the gang had shared this woman's favours? One of them? All of them? Together?

First thing tomorrow morning he would find out who she was and arrange for her to be deported. He didn't want to find her waiting for him a second time, he told himself savagely. He wasn't going to risk another night like tonight. Nor did he want to have to share his bed with her. But, since she was already deeply asleep in it… He looked towards the bedroom door. He had converted the second bedroom into an office, and the furniture in the living room was not conducive to a decent night's sleep. Anyway, why the hell should he give up his right to sleep in his own comfortable king-sized bed because it already had an occupant?

He reached for the covers.

Sunlight pouring through the unshuttered windows slanted gold bars across Gwynneth's face, its heat drawing her reluctantly from sleep. Unfamiliar images and sensations curled like autumn smoke through her thoughts and her body, making her frown in rejection and try to ignore the way her heartbeat picked up.

Cautiously she opened her eyes, exhaling in relief when she found that she was lying in the same bed she had originally gone to sleep in last night—and, more importantly, she was lying there alone. But she had not slept there alone during the night, she recognised, her face starting to burn as she saw the telltale imprint of another head on the pillow next to hers. So last night had not just been a fevered dream or a trick of her imagination.

She pushed back the covers and swung her feet onto the floor, tensing as she did so. She certainly wasn't imagining the small bruises on her skin where hard hands had held her. She wasn't imagining either the heavy fullness of her breasts or the sensitivity of her nipples. There was an unfamiliar ache deep inside her. Of fulfillment? Or of longing for what she had not had? A longing for *more* of what she had had, for the satisfaction of being totally and completely sexually possessed?

She shook her head, trying to disperse the images that clung to her mind as betrayingly as the scent of him still clung to her skin.

She had no idea what had caused last night's aberration in her behaviour, the total deviation from the controlled pathway she normally imposed on it. She could come up with a variety of theories, though, ranging from mundane jet lag to some kind of delayed reaction to her father's death.

Since she did not know what had been responsible for the way she had acted, the best thing she could do now, she told herself sturdily, was to put the entire incident behind her and refuse to give in to the self-indulgence of spending time and energy focusing on it. Like anything else, once starved of energy it would quickly shrivel to nothing.

But the man who had shared the wild passion of the night

with her—who was he? How had he got into the apartment? Logic suggested that he must have a key, which further suggested that he must be employed to look after the apartments in some capacity. Was what had happened last night a regular occurrence? Something he considered to be a perk of the job? If so, she had had a very lucky escape. She shuddered to think now of the kind of health risks she had run in coming so close to unprotected sex with a stranger. Why hadn't she stopped him?

Inside her head she could hear her own voice, taunting her that she was after all her parents' daughter, and that all the years of struggling to deny the fact, to reject it and prove to herself she could never be caught in the trap of her father's sexuality, had been swept away by her physical desire for a stranger.

Her parents' marriage had been the result of her father's uncontrollable sexuality and her mother's equally out-of-control emotional neediness. In a word: lust. She had sworn she would never be like them.

So what had happened?

She didn't drink, and she most certainly didn't do drugs, so she couldn't blame either of them.

She walked into the bathroom and turned on the shower. As she had already told herself, she couldn't change what had happened, but she could refuse to dwell on it or endlessly analyse it. She could choose to ignore it, to seal it off and lock it away where she would never need to think about it again. And, thankfully, there was no reason why she would have to think about it again.

In three days' time she would be back in London, having arranged for ownership of the apartment to be put in her name and having put it up for sale.

She just hoped it would sell quickly. Her plan was that once

the apartment had been sold she would have all the money put
into a trust fund for Anthony and Teresa. They were both her
late father's responsibility after all. Teresa was little more
than a girl and Anthony was his son.

Gwynneth dried herself quickly, ignoring the small marks
on her body that were evidence of last night's passion. A mental
image of herself raking a tanned male shoulder with her teeth,
clawing a male back in hunger, flashed through her mind.
Defensively she dipped her head, hurrying to get herself some
clean clothes. As she left the room, she hesitated. What if he
was still here somewhere in the apartment, waiting….? Waiting
for what? A repeat of last night? Her belly clenched fiercely
around the distinctive and very betraying surge of hot excitement that stirred inside her. He wasn't here, she told herself.
Instinctively she knew that. Taking a deep breath, she opened
the bedroom door and stepped resolutely into the hallway.

Half an hour later, having been delighted to find some coffee
in a kitchen that was otherwise bare of provisions, she was
ready to leave for her appointment. Picking up her handbag,
she frowned as she saw the thick wad of Zurani currency
stuffed into her passport. How had that got there? Uneasily
she removed the money from her handbag, her eyes widening
as she saw the note that was with it. The words *To professional
services for last night* were written firmly on the paper, and
it was abundantly plain just what they meant.

Automatically she stiffened in angry rejection of both the
meaning of the note and her own reaction to it. How could
she possibly feel hurt because a man who was a complete
stranger had made an error of judgement? Although even
though he was a stranger, it was a very insulting error of

judgement, she reminded herself shakily. After all, he was the one who had invaded her privacy and entered the apartment uninvited. Even so…

Hadn't she always believed that she had to be guardian of her own reputation and her own values? That she had to do everything she could to prevent herself being labelled as her father's daughter?

Maybe, but surely a woman could have sex with a man without being labelled a whore? By what right did a man who walked into an unknown woman's apartment and then had a sexual encounter with her assume she was selling the sex? By the right of being male? Did she really need to tell herself that? Wasn't it a given—something that all women instinctively understood? Outwardly things might have changed from the days when a woman's virtue and virginity were something to be prized, but inwardly they hadn't changed as much as people liked to think.

By leaving her money he was telling her brutally what he thought of her. She was a commodity he had bought and used. And having used her he was now discarding her.

Dry-eyed, but with her face burning and her heart hot with furious outrage, she left the apartment.

CHAPTER THREE

TARIQ frowned as he listened to the Ruler's Chief of Police deploring the fact that because they had not as yet discovered the identity of the Zurani who was working for the gang he could not give the order for the gang to be deported, after a warning of the very long prison sentence they would face if they were ever found in Zuran again.

Knowing that it was almost time for the Ruler to hold his regular monthly public *divan*—traditionally an opportunity for the Ruler's subjects to bring to him their problems and questions so that he might dispense with justice and answers—Tariq stood up and bowed formally to the Ruler, as did the Chief of Police.

On her way back to the apartment, following her appointment, Gwynneth had stopped off at a small supermarket to buy a few basic supplies. As she put these away in the empty cupboards and fridge freezer of the apartment it was what she had been told by the sympathetic young official she had met earlier that was occupying her thoughts.

It had never occurred to her that there might be a problem

registering her ownership of the apartment—especially since she had followed the advice she had been given by the Zurani Embassy in London and had brought with her documentation to prove her father's ownership of the apartment and to confirm her own identity. Fortunately, when her father had boasted to her about the apartment he had shown her the deeds and told her that he intended to deposit them with his London bank for safekeeping.

Now, though, it transpired that proving her father's ownership of the apartment was not going to be as straightforward as simply producing the deeds—as the charming official had explained to her, in an extremely grave tone of voice.

Her heart had sunk just about as low as she felt it could sink as she'd listened to him telling her about the double-selling scam that had resulted in two separate sets of buyers believing they had purchased the same property. And then had come the additional blow of hearing about the length of time it would take to make painstaking enquiries to establish who had been duped and who in fact did own a property.

'So what should I do now?' she had appealed.

'If you are able to do so, your best course of action would be to remain here in Zuran until we can establish whether or not your father owned the apartment.'

'I'm actually staying in the apartment,' Gwynneth had felt obliged to tell him, adding with concern, 'And I certainly can't afford to pay for a hotel. If there is another potential owner, then…'

'I shall make a note on the file to the effect that you are currently occupying the flat, but that you are aware of the issue of its ownership,' she had been told.

Now Gwynneth reached for her mobile and switched it on.

She would have to tell Teresa what had happened, but first she had another phone call to make.

As she pressed the speed dial for her boss's number she looked at her watch. It would be nine o'clock in the morning in the UK. Piers would have been at work for a while now. He was a workaholic who liked to be at his desk by eight.

He picked up the call within a couple of rings.

'Hi, Piers—it's Gwynneth,' she announced herself, smiling when she heard the warmth in his voice as he answered.

They had been working together for over a year, and Piers had made it plain that he wanted to put their relationship on a more personal footing. However, much as she liked him as a person, she had no desire for them to become a couple, and so had refused his offers to take her out as gently as she could.

Quickly she explained what was happening, exhaling in relief when he said immediately that she must stay in Zuran for as long as it took to get things sorted out.

'I know you aren't a clock-watcher, Gwynneth. You've put in a lot of extra hours these last few months, and I appreciate that. I'm going to miss you, though,' he told her softly. 'Pity I can't take some time off myself and fly out there to join you,' he added ruefully, before they ended their call.

Her duty to her employers dealt with, Gwynneth started to wonder if she ought to get in touch with the British Embassy in Zuran and get their opinion of the situation with regard to the apartment. But the young Zurani official had cautioned her not to discuss the matter with anyone, explaining that the Zurani authorities, whilst not responsible for the fraud in any way, were prepared to deal fairly and sympathetically with the victims providing they undertook not to fuel panic or potentially destructive rumours by talking publicly about what had happened.

Just how long would she have to stay here in Zuran before everything was sorted out? Long enough for last night's stranger to make a return visit? Immediately she stiffened in rejection of the feeling surging through her. She had told herself not to think about last night, or the man she had shared it with. It was over—gone—and for her own sake she should accept that.

But what if she didn't want to accept it? If she wanted…

What? A repeat performance? Was she totally crazy? She suddenly remembered that she still had the money he had left her in her handbag. Opening it, she removed the bundle of notes with trembling fingers. So much money. Even without counting it she could see that.

Money that Teresa and Anthony might need very badly if things went wrong and it turned out that the apartment wasn't her father's and the Zurani Government chose not to compensate her.

She dropped the notes onto the table as swiftly as though they were contaminated. If only she knew more. How long would she have to wait for that promised phone call?

She went into the kitchen and filled the kettle with water, having decided to make herself a cup of coffee before she spoke to Teresa, whom she knew would be anxiously waiting to hear from her.

He couldn't wait to get this whole wretched business sorted out, and the corrupt Zurani official unmasked, so that he could get on with his own life. A life that did not include in it a woman like Gwynneth Talbot, Tariq assured himself grimly, as he stepped out of the lift and slid the key card into the door of the apartment. He had such plans for the small desert kingdom he had inherited.

The discovery that an old legend attached to it, claiming that it had once been the site of some hanging gardens said to rival those of ancient Babylon, had actually been founded on fact had led to Tariq's decision to have the site of the original palace and its gardens excavated and if possible reconstructed. It was an ambitious and long-term plan, but one that would be richly rewarding, and Tariq was totally committed to its execution. The ongoing work on the project was already attracting the interest of both tourists and experts in the archaeological field.

Normally when Tariq was in Zuran he stayed either at the Palace or in his personal suite at one of the two hotels in which he had a financial interest. However, whenever he could he much preferred to spend his free time living simply in the desert, in one of the black tents of his mother's Bedouin ancestors. Bedouin tribesmen still travelled the old desert routes, although their numbers were dwindling now, and certain members of the Ruler's extended family had close connections with such tribes—as he did himself through his mother. Just thinking of the desert brought him a fierce longing for the feel of one of his fleet-footed Arabian horses beneath him as they raced together across the sands while dawn broke and the sun started to rise. Inside his head he could see the mental image his longing was creating. And he could see, too, the woman who rode at his side, her face turned towards his own, her green eyes brilliant with excitement for the desert and for him—

Tariq froze in furious rejection of the image that slipped so treacherously past his guard. The woman he would choose to share his life would *not* be that woman. Last night's woman. Gwynneth. He had seen her name in her passport when he had pushed the money into her bag this morning.

Gwynneth! The first thing Tariq heard when he walked into the apartment was the sound of her voice.

'There's a bit of a problem. But don't worry. I'll do whatever I have to do to make sure we get the money—just as I promised you I would, and no matter how long I have to stay here to get it or what I have to do.'

She was speaking grimly. As though she was trying to reassure someone. She was seated at the kitchen table with her back to him, the money he had left her this morning in an untidy pile beside her.

An uncomfortable mix of very powerful feelings was fighting for control of his emotions: righteous anger that she had dared to stay here when he had made it obvious that he wanted her to leave; and a deeper, darker feeling of savaged male pride at hearing her underline the fact that all he was to her was a source of income. The physical memories of last night were storming the defences he had put up against them like grains of sand chafing against his skin.

Gwynneth sighed as she ended her call to Teresa. She hadn't wanted to worry the younger girl by saying too much to her, even though she desperately wanted to have someone she could confide her own anxieties to. Her mind was still on Teresa and the problems of her father's apartment, but some sixth sense made her turn round, the colour momentarily leaving her face only to return in a hot wave of betraying soft pink awareness as she stood up shakily.

'*You!* You've come back!'

'Very dramatic—but somewhat ineffective, surely? Since you must have realised that I *would* come back.' Tariq responded curtly to her breathy gasp.

Had she? He had such a powerful air of authority about

him that for a moment she was almost in danger of believing him. Almost.

'Why would I do that?' she challenged him daringly.

'I should have thought that was obvious.'

Gwynneth couldn't help it. She could feel the colour burning up under her skin as her body reacted to what he had said. Her body couldn't actually be *pleased* that he had come back? That he wanted more of her? Could it? Surely that wasn't possible? She mustn't let it feel like that, she decided, panicking. What had happened last night was excusable—just—as an isolated, never to be repeated incident. So long as that was what it remained.

'After all,' Tariq continued, 'this does happen to be my apartment.'

His apartment? *His* apartment? She stared at him in shocked dismay. That couldn't possibly be true! Could it? A horrible cold feeling of uncertainty and dismay was creeping over her. What if it was true? If it was, then obviously he wasn't here because of her. He hadn't come back because he wanted a repeat performance of last night's sex, as she had so humiliatingly assumed.

If it was true— But it wasn't true. It couldn't possibly be true; she wasn't going to let it be true, she decided wildly, her normal facility for calm, rational, logical thinking disintegrating in the face of her emotional reaction to both him and his unwelcome information.

But worse was to come. As she struggled to assimilate his unwelcome news he added sharply, 'Since I've already added a generous bonus to what you were paid for last night—particularly generous under the circumstances—I fail to see why you are still here. Surely for a woman in your profession time is money? Or did you think I might be persuaded to keep you on for tonight as well?'

'Are you trying to suggest that I'm a prostitute?' Gwynneth demanded in disbelief.

'Are you trying to suggest that you aren't?' His voice was as derisive as the look in his eyes. 'Because if so you're wasting your time. I know what you are, why you were waiting in my bed for me, and who arranged for you to be there.'

'What? This is crazy!' Gwynneth protested shakily. 'Who—? Who—?'

'Stop right there. I don't want to hear another word. Pick up your money and go,' Tariq ordered, then frowned as his mobile—the one he used only for calls from the gang—started to ring.

'Wait,' he told Gwynneth contradictorily, striding out of the kitchen and closing the door behind him, leaving her inside.

'Get yourself down to the marina—pronto. Chad wants to see you—now.' The familiar voice of one of the gang members rasped in Tariq's ear.

The call was disconnected before he could make any response. He looked at the closed kitchen door. At this delicate stage in the proceedings he couldn't afford to antagonise the leader of the gang by refusing to obey him.

What on earth had she got herself into? Gwynneth worried anxiously. Suddenly she was seeing last night's uncharacteristic and admittedly very dangerous and foolish sexual adventure in a very different and sickeningly seedy and unpleasant light. She had been mistaken for a prostitute and she was about to be evicted from her own apartment. The situation she was in couldn't have been any worse. Could it? What about the fact that not so very long ago she had virtually caught herself wondering if last night's events might be repeated?

The kitchen door was opening.

Gwynneth took a deep breath.

'You've got this all wrong. I am *not* a prostitute.'

She certainly wasn't done up like one, Tariq acknowledged, unable to stop himself from looking not so much *at* her as *for* her, the moment he stepped into the kitchen. She wasn't wearing make-up, her clothes looked more suited to an office worker, and no man looking at her would feel that she was making any attempt to be alluring. And as for last night… He had been the one pleasuring her, not the other way around.

'I'd agree that you certainly aren't a good advertisement for your profession,' he agreed unkindly.

'Why won't you listen to me?' Gwynneth protested. 'I am not a prostitute! I'm—'

'An escort?' Tariq suggested silkily, and gave a condemnatory shrug. 'It doesn't matter what name you give what you do. It doesn't change the fact that you sell your body to men for their sexual pleasure. Do your family know what you do? Your father?' he demanded abruptly, without knowing why he should be asking her such a question—the kind of question that might almost suggest that he cared.

'My father is dead.'

So, like him, she was fatherless. That was no reason for him to feel the sudden surge of fellow feeling towards her, Tariq warned himself angrily.

'So is mine,' he told her coldly. 'That is no excuse. Surely there is some other way you could support yourself? Have you no pride? No self-respect? No—?'

'I don't need an excuse. And as for *me* not having any pride— what about you?' Gwynneth shot back, and took advantage of the sudden silence her attack had gained her to point out pithily, 'After all, you didn't exactly reject me, did you?'

What she was saying was perfectly true, but that didn't make it any easier to accept, Tariq admitted unwillingly.

He could almost feel her angry defiance burning through the air-conditioned chill of the small kitchen. No woman who lived as this one did had the right to look and behave as she was. She was positively exuding righteous indignation, forcing him to see and react to her as a human being and not a piece of human merchandise. He had to put an end to this dangerous emotional connection she had somehow brought to life between them. Apart from anything else, he was going to be late for his meeting on the yacht.

'You can stop right there,' he told Gwynneth, crossing the kitchen and taking hold of her arm before she could evade him.

Had he changed his mind? Was he, despite all he had said, going to drag her back to his bed right now and…? A shocking explicit thrill of female excitement shot through her, weakening her so much that she sagged slightly in his hold, leaning into him, her breasts pressing against the hardness of his arm. Without even having to think about it she leaned closer and harder, closing her eyes the better to relish her own pleasure at the sensual contact between her flesh and his. And in that hot darkness she was immediately transported back to the arousal-drenched hours of the previous night, complete with faithful audio as well as visual record.

Tariq looked down into the face turned up towards his own. Her eyes were closed and her lips were open; even her skin seemed to shimmer with sensual luminosity. He had been wrong, he realised savagely as he felt his own body react to her. She was not just good at her chosen profession. She was exceptional. He couldn't remember any woman arousing him either so immediately or so intensely—and certainly not both at the same time. His fingers bit into the softness of her arm as he made to shake her off, but still he couldn't drag his gaze from the temptation of her parted lips. Nor could he stop himself from wanting to reach out and fill his free hand with the weight of one of the soft warm breasts she had pressed so deliberately and enticingly against his arm. Was it because of last night that he was having so much trouble rejecting the images his mind was conjuring up? Because of how she had made him feel then that he wanted her so immediately and fiercely now?

Despite the coolness of the kitchen Tariq could feel sweat dampening his flesh whilst his mind raced with the turmoil of his emotions.

'Forget it,' he told her brutally, and pushed her away, keeping only a tight hold on one wrist.

Gwynneth's eyes snapped open, and she sucked in a distressed breath as reality crashed back down. 'Forget what?' she demanded, recouping. 'Forget that you've insulted me—verbally, physically and emotionally?' The numbing effect of her original shock and his sensual appeal had worn off now, leaving her sick with fury and disbelief.

'Forget those unsubtle plans you're hatching for tonight,' he corrected her. 'Because I'm telling you now, you won't be spending it my bed.'

No, she wouldn't. Because it wasn't *his* bed. It was hers, and she had the documents to prove it—or at least she hoped she did. She didn't have anywhere else to stay, and she certainly wasn't going to be bullied into moving out of the apartment by a man who had mistaken her for a prostitute!

'Let go of me!'

For a moment she thought he was going to ignore her, that instead he would pull her close to him again and...

The angry hiss of his breath as he exhaled told her she was wrong.

'I have to go out now,' he told her flatly. 'And you had better not be here when I get back.' The last thing he wanted was to be seen leaving the apartment with a woman of her type—otherwise he would have physically removed her himself.

And how will you do that? a small, cynical inner voice mocked him. *Via the bedroom?*

Silencing it, he continued, 'If you are, then I shall inform the police of your presence and your profession. And since, as I am sure you already know, prostitution is against the law in Zuran, you will be deported and refused future entry to the country.'

Now, abruptly, fear was crawling through her veins and locking onto her anger, feeding off its strength and smothering it.

'You can't do that,' she protested, adding emotionally, 'You're making a mistake!'

Tariq's mouth compressed. 'No. You are the one who is doing that.'

Gwynneth swung away from him to conceal her expression. Thinking that she was going to walk out on him, Tariq stepped in front of her. Immediately it was as though they were locked together inside an invisible bubble of sensual tension—or so it seemed to Gwynneth as she tried to make her lungs work properly and her heart slow to its normal rate. She couldn't seem to look anywhere but at the man standing in front of her, to do anything but remember last night—feel anything but the intense arousal that she was feeling.

What was it about her that had this effect on him? Tariq wondered savagely. At no time in the whole of his life had he wanted to take hold of any woman and kiss her until the only words her lips could frame were his name and a plea for more.

Hold me…touch me…make me yours. Gwynneth could feel the words pounding through her veins with every thud of her heartbeat, filling her mind and her senses. So much so that she felt as though they were written into her flesh. Her angry pride fought with the liquid heat of her desire and was overwhelmed by it as it flooded over the rigid barriers trickling through every tiny hole it could find to reunite in a fast-flowing surge that took her across the no man's land that was the space between them and into the heat zone of Tariq's body. She could sense the command going from his brain to his muscles to lift his arms so that they could enfold her. And once they had…

There was a ringing sound inside her head. No, not inside her head. The noise was coming from the mobile Tariq was lifting to his ear as he turned away from her. Who was calling him? A woman? Something previously unknown and darkly dangerous ripped at her emotions.

'Where are you? You were supposed to be at the marina ten minutes ago.'

'I've been delayed,' Tariq answered, looking briefly at Gwynneth and wondering how much she was being paid to spy on him as well as go to bed with him before he added coolly, 'Chad will understand why when I explain.'

'You'd better hope he does. Otherwise you're going to be in big trouble. Get yourself down here, double-quick.'

There was no time for him to argue with Gwynneth. Nor to do anything else with her either. Like what? There wasn't *anything* he wanted to do with her.

Liar, an inner voice goaded him as he opened the kitchen door. He ignored it as he paused to warn her, 'Remember what I told you. When I get back I don't want to find you here. If you are, you know what you can expect.'

CHAPTER FOUR

GWYNNETH tottered over to the table and sank down thankfully into one of the chairs. Her legs felt boneless, her heart was racing, her forehead was damp with sweat and her mouth was dry. Classic signs of fear—or sexual excitement.

What on earth was happening to her? A man—a stranger—a naked stranger—walked into her bedroom, and instead of screaming for help she went to bed with him. That same man accused her of being a prostitute and she still let herself be aroused by him. *Let* herself? Since when, in the whole of this nightmarish scenario, had what purported to be the thinking, reasoning part of her had any say in *anything*? Why hadn't she insisted on him listening to her? Why hadn't she made him understand just how wrong he was?

She would have to inform the young man who was trying to help her what had happened. Well, at least some of what had happened, she amended mentally. Why hadn't she insisted on *him*, her co-owner, giving her his name? That way at least she would have had something concrete to pass on to the authorities. Was he the rightful owner of the apartment or was she?

She looked for her handbag. It was on the worktop. She

found the card the young official had given her and tapped his phone number into her mobile.

He answered her call almost immediately. Introducing herself, she asked anxiously if he remembered their meeting, exhaling in relief when he assured her that he did. Quickly she told him what had happened.

'You say this man claims that he too is the owner of the apartment?' the young official questioned.

'That's what he said,' Gwynneth confirmed unhappily.

'We have no record as yet of anyone else lodging a claim against this apartment,' he assured her.

'So that means that I am in the clear to stay here, does it?' Gwynneth pressed him.

'Certainly,' he agreed promptly. 'We know that your apartment block is one of those involved in this unfortunate fraud, but as yet no one else has come forward to claim ownership of your particular apartment. However, as I explained to you, that does not mean another potential owner does not exist,' he cautioned.

'But until they actually present themselves to you and make a legal claim the apartment is notionally at least mine?'

'You are certainly free to make use of it until such time as we have ascertained who in fact *does* own it,' he corrected her gently.

Well, at least that meant that she didn't have to give in to *his* bullying, Gwynneth reassured herself later, in an attempt to quell the anxiety that was causing her to feel so on edge.

He might believe he had the upper hand, with his threats to tell the police about her and have her deported, but he was the one who was going to look foolish when he was forced to accept the truth. And she was going to make sure that he *did* accept it, Gwynneth decided vigorously. No matter what it took. No way was *any* man going to be allowed to make the kind of assumptions about her *he* had made, without her defending herself from them.

It felt bittersweet now to look back on her waking moments this morning and her dread that he might have realised how new she was to everything they had shared, and that from that he might have thought that he was something—someone—special. Ridiculously, she had even begun her defence against that. How naïve she had been, believing that all she had to protect herself from was a choice between two fears: one, that she had inherited her father's sexuality, the other that somehow or other in touching her flesh *he* had also touched her heart. She had thought then in her naïveté that nothing could be worse than being forced to defend herself with one of these two choices. But now she knew better.

How could he possibly believe that what had happened between them last night had been motivated on her part by money? Surely he had to have been able to see that she wasn't like that—that she couldn't cold-bloodedly sell her flesh for some man to use whilst she distracted herself from what he was doing by counting up the financial benefit she was going to gain. Behind her anger and her disbelief, and her fears about the apartment and the future of Teresa and Anthony, there was also a growing feeling of shocked misery and pain.

She wanted her self-respect back; she wanted back the person she had been before *him*. And as for her leaving the apartment—no way was she going anywhere. Not now.

'Ah, Tariq. Good. I'm glad you're here…finally.'

Chad Rheinvelt's smile and voice were as smooth as the satin skin of the half-naked girl he was caressing as he lounged in his chair in the main cabin of the luxurious yacht. Several other members of the gang were also in the cabin, standing with their arms folded across their chests or slouching against the cabin walls. Bully boys, heavies, enforcers—it didn't matter what label you put on them, their appearance made it obvious what they were, Tariq reflected grimly.

'I've got a job for you,' Chad told him. He had slipped his hand into the girl's skimpy top and she was now squirming in supposed delight as he played with her breast whilst his men looked on.

The girl he was fondling might easily have been Gwynneth.

Tariq's raw, savage emotional response to that knowledge caught him off guard. What the hell was he doing, allowing himself to react like this to a woman who sold her body to any man who could afford to buy it?

'You've told us all about your high status in Zuran. Here's your chance to prove it. I need official sanction for a few friends of mine to make a long-term stay in Zuran—no questions asked. And I need it quickly.'

'A few friends?' Tariq questioned.

Chad turned to the girl, who was now sliding one slim brown hand along his inner thigh, her tongue-tip pressed wetly against her bottom lip. Tariq could feel his belly curling with contempt and revulsion.

'Jeni here is one of them. Fancy her? Regretting that you turned down my offer to send her to you now, are you? Your loss. She's pretty good. The girls who work for me are all tried out first by one of us, and if they're especially good they might be lucky enough to have a few of us put them through their paces—eh, Jeni?' Chad was laughing as he tweaked her nipple, his erection straining openly against the cloth of his shorts.

Had he misunderstood what Chad had just said? Tariq replayed the words very carefully and slowly inside his head.

'Well, don't worry. There's plenty more where Jeni comes from if you change your mind. Or at least there will be once you do your stuff for us. How long will it take a man in your position to get this sorted, Tariq?'

Somehow Tariq managed to drag his thoughts away from the enormity of what he had just heard and focus them instead on the open challenge he was being given. As a test? Or as a trap?

'How long is a piece of string?' he responded, as carelessly as he could. 'I can make it possible for the girls to enter Zuran immediately.' That was certainly true. He gave a small shrug. 'But for me to do so without causing any questions to be asked or arousing any suspicions may take a little time.'

Chad was listening to him in silence. Had they somehow found out the truth about him? But, after a pause that Tariq felt was too long, Chad inclined his head and gave a small nod.

'Okay, you've got that time. But I want to be kept fully informed. Oh, and be warned. There isn't any room in this organisation for those who can't keep their promises.'

Was that merely a warning to him? Or an allusion to the Zurani official who was working on the fraudulent property scam with him? It would be impossible for anyone else to get permission for Chad's prostitutes to so much as enter the country, never mind work there as he plainly intended them to do. Even Tariq couldn't have done so other than as part of his current undercover operation.

He was strongly tempted to ask directly about the other Zurani national who was in Chad's pay. But that would, he knew, risk the whole operation. The urge only underlined how impatient he was to be free to walk away from the whole sordid affair. He needed to wait, to earn Chad's trust, before he could start digging for his criminal countryman's identity.

There was something he *could* ask, though.

'Are any of the girls actually working here yet?' he asked Chad as carelessly as he could.

'I'm not that much of a fool,' Chad told him. 'I've paid good money for them—they're clean, well taught, stunning to look at, not your out-of-the-gutter, everyone's-already-had-it tat. No way am I going to risk losing my investment by letting them work until I've got an official okay. Jeni and a few more are here on the yacht to show to certain special customers whom I can trust and who might want to prebook their services. No way do they go anywhere without my say-so, and one of my men is keeping a watch on them. The rest of them are in a safe house outside the country, and I've got a bunch of guys making sure they stay there. Do you want to have a look at the rest of them?'

Tariq nodded his head.

Five minutes later, six stunningly beautiful young women were lined up in front of him. Six totally unfamiliar young women. Not one of them was Gwynneth, and it was plain that if one of his expensive properties were missing Chad would know about it.

'If you like, you can have Jeni tonight. I'll get one of the guys to bring her over to your place for a couple of hours and then bring her back. Or you can have a couple of hours here with her now? Premium rates apply, though.' Chad laughed.

Tariq shook his head. 'Not right now. There are people I need to speak to with regard to what we've just been discussing,' he told him truthfully.

* * *

Gwynneth stiffened defensively as she heard Tariq come in, her mouth dry as she stared at the locked door of the study. The room had obviously been intended to be used as a bedroom but someone—him, no doubt—had furnished it as an office, with a desk and a computer, a small sofabed and a shelf of books. One of them in particular had caught her eye, because it was a history of Zuran. Under normal circumstances she would have felt tempted to pick it up and read it.

Her heart was pounding. She had discovered that this small room had a lock on it when she had explored the apartment after Tariq had gone, and she had decided to lock herself inside it to await his return. That way at least she could stop him from forcibly evicting her from the apartment—although the small study with its equally small *en suite* bathroom was now beginning to feel slightly claustrophobic.

Tariq looked around the apparently empty flat. Had she taken him at his word and left? He discovered that he wasn't as pleased by that thought as he ought to have been. His overdeveloped sense of duty was making him want to see a neat and tidy end to events, rather than having to worry about what a young woman as reckless as Ms Gwynneth Talbot might get herself involved with next.

He could still smell her scent on the air—prim, light and delicate. He strode into the kitchen and saw the handbag and mobile phone on the counter with some relief. She was clearly still here. He walked over to them and removed Gwynneth's passport from her bag.

He frowned as he heard a small rustle of sound. It was coming from his office.

'Gwynneth?'

Her tension increased when she heard him calling her

name, but not because she was alarmed this time. No, the tension tightening through her body had a very different cause. Images flashed through her head—a large bed, a satin-skinned naked male body, knowing hands whose touch she could still feel on her own flesh.

Tariq stalked over to the office, and cursed under his breath when he realised that she had locked herself in.

'Open this door!' he demanded.

'You have no right to tell me to do anything,' Gwynneth called back. 'You may think that you own this apartment, but I have the paperwork to prove that my father believed he owned it too. Now he's dead, and it's mine. And I'm not going to be bullied or threatened into walking out of it and leaving you in sole possession. This is a very valuable property, and until someone proves that it isn't mine I'm going to stay right here, where I can make sure no one can take it away from me.'

She was proud of the firmness in her voice, and proud too of the words she had been rehearsing so carefully.

So she wasn't a prostitute. But money was obviously important to her—very important, if she was prepared to stay here after the accusations he had made against her, Tariq thought scathingly. There had been no emotion whatsoever in her voice when she had spoken of her father's death.

'We need to talk properly about this,' he advised her.

'I've already tried to do that,' Gwynneth reminded him. 'But you wouldn't listen. For all I know everything you've said and done from the moment I walked into the apartment could be part of some plan you've hatched to try and get me to leave the country so that you can claim this place.'

'You're being ridiculous.'

'Am I? You obviously have a key for this place, just as I do. You've got to know about this double-selling fraud that's been going on, but you haven't registered your interest with the authorities as I've done. I've checked up on that! Why not?' she challenged him. 'If you genuinely believe the apartment to be yours then that is the first thing you would have done. I think you are some kind of opportunist, and this place isn't yours at all. You must have been over the moon when you discovered your only rival for ownership was me.' It was heaven being able to speak her mind to him like this, knowing that she was safely out of his reach.

'So you're going to stay in there and starve, are you?' Tariq demanded. 'The legal process here in Zuran is notoriously long-winded.'

Food! She hadn't thought of that in her relief at discovering she could lock him out.

'A human being can live for weeks just on water.'

'Some can—certain members of the Bedouin tribe amongst them—but I doubt you could. Besides, I have a spare key to the study.'

Gwynneth looked at the door.

'I'm not a prostitute,' she warned him.

Tariq exhaled impatiently.

'No, I realise that now.'

'What? How? Why?' Why was she sounding as though she was grateful to him for accepting what was, after all, the truth? 'I could report you to the authorities for what you've done—and said,' she said, attempting menace.

'Not from in there you can't,' Tariq told her succinctly. 'My computer is locked and you left your mobile in the kitchen—along with your handbag.' While he had been talking to her he had also been punching into his own mobile the hotline number to Zuran's Chief of Police. He now had enough information on Gwynneth to get a full report on her. He walked away from the study and into the kitchen, putting her passport back into her bag as he passed it and shutting the door behind him, so that he could instruct the Chief to find out everything he could about her.

'Oh, and I think it could be worthwhile checking to see if anyone within the government has been making enquiries about the possibility of bringing fifty or so young women into the country. Chad Rheinvelt has asked me to make it possible for him to import a group of prostitutes to work in Zuran. I've had to pretend to agree to do what he's asked, but I've warned him it could take time.'

Gwynneth listened to the muffled sounds of speech and reflected on her situation. She had no food, no mobile, no means of contacting the outside world. He had at least accepted that she wasn't a prostitute. Didn't it therefore make sense for her to unlock the door and talk to him face-to-face?

Tariq heard the key turning in the lock as he opened the kitchen door. Impassively he stood and waited for Gwynneth to come out.

It was unfortunate that she was so determined to lay claim to the apartment. Not that he wanted it. However, whilst he was obliged to masquerade as a disaffected member of Zuran's ruling family, motivated by resentment and greed, he had no option but to stay here. Chad was a wily operator, a man who did not trust anyone easily. And to leave the apartment would inevitably arouse his suspicions.

Neither could he have his own interest in the apartment legally registered. That would lead to all manner of complications, and potentially increase the risk of him being unmasked. If anything, it was even more important now that Tariq should lull Chad into a false sense of security until they found out the identity of the Zurani in Chad's pay. He had to be unmasked before he and Chad found some way of perverting the law to enable Chad to bring his drug and prostitution rackets into Zuran. The international damage that would do to the credibility of the Ruler, and through him to Zuran itself, was incalculable. Zuran had a reputation to maintain, as a safe and law-abiding country, and it was on that reputation that its future success as an international tourist destination was based.

As Gwynneth stepped out and walked through to join him in the kitchen, Tariq's first thought was that somehow she looked smaller and more vulnerable than the image of her he had been carrying around in his mind.

It was difficult for her to lift her head and look him in the eye after not just what that happened but also what he had said and thought about her, but somehow Gwynneth managed to do so.

'So,' Tariq began, 'let me get this straight. You believe that your father owned this apartment?'

'No, I *know* that he owned it,' Gwynneth corrected him smartly. 'And I've got the papers to prove it.'

Ignoring that, Tariq asked, 'When did your father die?'

'Almost three weeks ago.'

'You mean you've waited as long as that to come here and claim your inheritance?' Tariq didn't bother to keep the contempt out of his voice.

Gwynneth's face started to burn, but before she could justify her behaviour by explaining about Teresa and Anthony his mobile started to ring. Tariq was looking at her in silence, waiting for her response. He continued to look at her, despite his ringing mobile, and the grim resoluteness of his concentration forced Gwynneth to look away as he finally answered it.

'Wait here,' he commanded, turning to walk out of the kitchen and closing the door behind him.

Tariq's caller was the Chief of Police, who was ringing to give him the information he had gathered on Gwynneth. He explained that she had taken leave from her job in the City of London to come to Zuran because she believed she had inherited an apartment purchased by her late father.

'Since this apartment is one of those involved in the recent double-selling fraud, she has been told that there could be a delay in establishing ownership. It seems she is anxious to register the property in her own name and then sell it as quickly as she can. She has been told, of course, about the Zurani compensation programme that is in force for victims of this fraud.'

'And she is legitimately the daughter and heir of this man?' Tariq demanded.

'The papers she produced were all in order,' the Chief of Police assured him.

'And this job in the City of London—what exactly is it?'

'She works as a financial analyst.'

'And that is her only source of income?' he persisted.

'Yes, as far as we know.'

Thanking the other man for the information he had obtained for him, Tariq ended the call and looked towards the closed door.

He had made a serious error of judgement. And that, for a man with his sense of pride and honour, was something he found very hard to bear. Even worse, he had allowed his emotions to conceal the truth from him in the same way that the silken veils of a dancing girl could obscure her body. A man watching her dance would be intoxicated and dazzled by the swirling colours and patterns of the silk, just as *he* had allowed himself to be deceived by the swirling mists of his anger. He had seen a naked woman and he had told himself that she was there to offer herself to him.

But that did not mean that he had to blame himself for what had happened. She had not attempted to stop him or to protest, had she? She had not behaved in any way that might have warned him he had made an error of judgement. She had not said or done anything to suggest that having sex with a stranger was not something she did regularly. But then, according to what he had heard, some modern young women were what he considered to be sexually promiscuous—although they did not see it that way. They boasted openly of one-night stands, and worse! And, that being the case, why should he berate himself for taking what she had given? He owed her nothing.

CHAPTER FIVE

TARIQ opened the door and strode back into the kitchen.

Gwynneth watched him with a small quiver of sensation gripping her stomach. It was ridiculous, she knew, but she was forced to admit that there was something about the sight of a tall, forbiddingly imposing man dressed in flowing white robes that triggered a dangerous and previously unknown reaction in her. Or was it just *this* man who caused that reaction? The question slipped under her guard before she could deflect it, leaving her feeling agitated and angrily defensive as she fought to deny that her reaction was based on anything personal.

'So, if you believe that your father owned this apartment, why didn't you say anything about it last night?'

It took Gwynneth several precious seconds to dismiss the effect he was having on her and to gather up the threads of their previous discussion.

'When?' she answered. 'You hardly gave me the chance. I thought I was alone in the apartment, and then I thought you had broken in, and...'

Tariq gave her a derisory look.

'Everything happened so quickly,' she defended herself.

'And you are a woman who has a hunger for money and

no doubt thought that by going to bed with me you might be able to acquire a little more—perhaps in the form of a gift of some sort?'

'No!' Gwynneth denied sharply. But it wasn't true, was it? She *had* deep down inside, with that part of her she never normally allowed to surface, wanted a gift from him—the gift of her own sexual fulfilment via wild, passionate and abandoned sexual intimacy. 'I was just—taken by surprise.'

'So why, then, once you were over the shock of my presence, didn't you stop me?'

'I…I didn't know what to think.'

She hadn't stopped him because she hadn't been capable of doing so—hadn't wanted to do so. Because she had entered a state of physical delight that had totally overwhelmed any kind of rationality, where self-denial had been the last thing on her mind.

The look he was giving her made her face burn hotly.

'I was half asleep,' she defended herself. 'I hardly knew what was happening, never mind *why* it was happening.'

She couldn't tell him about her past, about her father. And she certainly couldn't tell him about the repression of her own sexuality, or the fact that in some unfathomable way he had been the key that had turned the lock to release that pent-up sensuality. How could she possibly explain that to him when she could not understand it herself? And besides, if she did he might take it as a sign that…

That what? That she was vulnerable to him? That she might want to repeat what had happened? That she might want *him*? Well, she didn't. And even if she had done she would not have allowed herself to go on doing so, Gwynneth assured herself fiercely.

Another man might have been fooled and flattered into succumbing to that note of emotional vulnerability in the soft shakiness of her voice, Tariq acknowledged. But he was not that other man. He was not so easily taken in.

Not mentally or emotionally, maybe, but what about physically? What about the way he had reacted to her last night, and then again earlier today? That had not been the reaction of a man who was fully in control of himself and his body, had it?

It irked him that he had to subject himself to such inner questioning and probing, and he gave Gwynneth a look of razor-sharp cynicism, his voice cutting and arrogant.

'But this morning, when you found the note I had left, the money, you must have realised—'

That flash of disdain in the cool grey eyes, accompanied by a dismissive downward curl of the mouth that only last night had so hungrily tasted her own, infuriated Gwynneth.

'I must have realised what? That you are the kind of man who regards women as a commodity, to be bought and used and then discarded?' she challenged him with angry heat. 'Yes, I did realise that. And I told myself that once I had put in hand all the necessary paperwork to transfer my father's apartment into my own name I would try to find out how you had managed to gain access to the apartment so that I could ensure you couldn't do so again.' She gave a very creditable imitation of his own earlier contemptuous shrug. 'Of course, one knows that men like you exist—men who are so inadequate emotionally and mentally that they are unable to have a normal relationship with a woman, and by "normal" I mean one based on real feelings and true respect—but I would never have willingly debased myself by having a relationship with such a man.'

'We did not have a relationship,' Tariq interrupted her icily. 'We had a night in bed.'

'*We?* What we?' Gwynneth countered wildly. 'There was no "we" involved. You used my body to gain sexual gratification, and then you—'

'Are you seriously trying to tell me that you found no pleasure in what we shared?' Tariq interrupted ominously. 'Because if you are—'

'So you get off on turning women on sexually,' Gwynneth flashed back. 'That doesn't alter the fact that you have to pay to do it!'

'*Have* to?'

No one, never mind a woman, had ever spoken to or looked at Tariq with contempt. He was a member of the ruling house of Zuran, and, more than that, he was the sole descendant of a noble house of great antiquity—the living, breathing reality of a royal name born out of mystery and legend. He possessed incalculable wealth; he was used to being treated with respect and deference; he considered himself to be a stringently moral man. Had anyone suggested to him even two nights ago that he would lose himself so completely in lust that he would take to his bed a woman of dubious morals he would have vehemently denied that he could ever do such a thing.

And now, to have this woman accusing him as she had just done, and with the contempt she had just shown, dug into his pride like the talons of a falcon tearing at its prey to leave its bloodied entrails spilling out onto the hot sand.

He wanted—no, *needed* to take hold of her and punish her for what she had said, for what she was making him feel.

'I do not *have* to pay any woman to give herself to me. As

I am more than happy to prove to you—right now,' he informed her grimly

Gwynneth fell back as Tariq strode purposefully towards her. But it wasn't fear that was turning her belly liquid as she wrenched her overheated gaze from his mouth and searched wildly for some way to disperse the sexual tension invading the small space.

He wanted her! How could that be? Furious with himself, Tariq stepped back from her, half turning away to conceal the evidence of his arousal as he demanded, 'Since you are now aware that I too consider this apartment to be my property, presumably you have informed the authorities accordingly?'

Gwynneth slid her tongue-tip over her suddenly dry lips. 'Not as such,' she said. Silence greeted her admission, and she filled it with defensive speech. 'It isn't up to *me* to register your interest—and anyway how could I? I don't even know your name. I did say that there was someone who believed they might own it, but the authorities said that no one else had registered any interest.'

'And of course that pleased you. Especially since you can expect to gain an additional bonus because of the rise in value of the apartment since your father purchased it.'

'And why not?' Gwynneth retorted angrily.

Tariq remained silent, leaning back against the doorframe and folding his arms. Where the sleeve of his robe had fallen back Gwynneth could see the tanned bare flesh of his forearm, sinewy and muscular and possessed of a strength she had seen last night, when he had lifted her and held her.

A treacherous physical memory of sensual pleasure gripped her achingly. Immediately she banished it.

'If you *really* believe this apartment is yours, then why haven't you registered your interest yourself?' she asked him, making it plain that she didn't believe his claim.

Tariq had had enough. 'Do you dare to accuse me of lying?' he demanded incredulously.

Gwynneth could see how much her deliberate insult had angered him. She could feel how that anger was filling the enclosed space in a wave of hostile tension. She flinched as Tariq unfolded his arms, half expecting him to take hold of her and demonstrate his anger physically, but to her relief he remained where he was. The look he was giving her, though, said that he had seen and relished her fear, and for Gwynneth that in itself was a form of punishment. But she wasn't going to give in—either to it or to him. Until she was officially told that her father had not owned the apartment, she was staying right where she was.

'Don't think I haven't worked out what all this is about,' she told him. 'You're trying to bully me into leaving. But I'm not going. We have a saying in England—possession is nine-tenths of the law—'

'We have a similar belief here,' he interrupted her.

'You mean you intend to stay here as well?' Gwynneth didn't even attempt to conceal her dismay.

'I have as much right to do so as you. Probably even more,' Tariq told her truthfully.

Now what had she done? She didn't want to back down, but the last thing she wanted to have to do was share the apartment with him and risk a repetition of last night. When she had thrown that challenge at him it simply hadn't occurred to her that he would retaliate in kind. But she couldn't back out now just because of the images crowding into her head,

Gwynneth warned herself. She had Teresa and baby Anthony to think about.

'I'm staying. It's what my father would have wanted me to do.'

'And he meant a lot to you, obviously. After all, his death left you so grief-stricken that you spent virtually three whole weeks grieving for him before coming out here to claim your inheritance.'

Tariq waited for her to deny his charge and to fake crocodile tears, but to his surprise she simply said quietly, 'No, we didn't have a particularly close relationship. My parents divorced when I was eight. I hardly saw my father after that until I was in my late teens. Neither he nor my mother really wanted me.'

Tariq started to frown. Was this the reason for her focus on material wealth? Or was she trying to gain his sympathy?

'So who brought you up?'

Gwynneth smiled mirthlessly.

'I was brought up in a very expensive boarding school, paid for by my stepfather. Neither he nor my mother wanted to be reminded that she had once been married to my father. My stepfather is a very wealthy man, so when he returned to Australia with my mother I was left behind in England. It was easy enough to pay someone else to take over the responsibility for me.'

Tariq looked away from her. He too had attended an English boarding school, and experienced the loneliness that brought.

'But my childhood was a long time ago and in the past,' Gwynneth said lightly. 'This is the present. My father had a peripatetic lifestyle. This apartment is virtually his only financial asset, and as his daughter—'

'You want your blood money?' Tariq suggested unkindly.

'I want what is right and just.' Gwynneth sidestepped the question neatly. She had already answered far too many questions, told him far too much about herself. Oddly, given their relationship, she didn't want to reveal her father's weaknesses—but, as she quickly discovered, Tariq had an even more uncomfortable question for her to answer.

'Is that why you have sex with men you don't know? Because you see it as a way of getting back at your parents for your childhood?'

'I don't—' *I don't have sex full-stop*, she had been about to say, but stopped herself in time, saying instead, 'I don't have to explain myself to you. All you need to know is that I am going to stay here in this apartment until ownership of it is resolved, and nothing is going to change my mind. So, like I've just said, if you are planning to browbeat and bully me into leaving, you are wasting your time.'

This was a wholly untenable situation, but he had no option other than to accept it. And with it her presence here in the apartment.

For only that reason? Was he sure about that? Was he sure that his decision, his determination to stay at the apartment, didn't have anything to do with last night and the fact that a part of him could still taste her, still hear her, still feel her in his arms, body-to-body with his own flesh?

He wasn't a boy, he was thirty-four years old, but though he had a man's needs he also had self-control. He'd had the occasional liaison with an understanding, experienced woman, but he felt nothing but contempt for the gold-digging females who went from one man to another.

He could, of course, marry. But his parents' marriage had

left him cynically wary of such a commitment. They might have claimed to be deeply in love with one another when they had married, but that love had not lasted. His father had walked out on both his wife and son when Tariq had been a mere four years old. Tariq could still remember how devastated he had been, and the tears he had wept. The experience had left him wary of ever being governed by his emotions. Emotional celibacy was something he had deliberately chosen. Physical celibacy was more of a state he had moved into by default rather than choice, but it was a state he preferred to any of the other options available to him.

'If you want to stay—'

'What I want is for you to leave,' Gwynneth burst out. 'And the sooner the better. We can't both stay here,' she added, when he made no response. 'For one thing, there's only one bedroom.'

'*My* bedroom,' Tariq agreed. 'Or were you hoping that I might invite you to share it with me?

'After last night?'

It was the wrong thing to have said.

'I don't recall hearing you complain. In fact—'

'I've had enough of this,' Gwynneth told him fiercely, almost running out of the kitchen.

Her heart was pumping and her whole body was protesting at the strain she was imposing on it. It was almost evening and she had no idea where the day had gone. Her head was throbbing almost as much as her heart was pounding. She needed some fresh air—and a breathing space, she acknowledged, but she dared not go out just in case he managed by some Machiavellian means to prevent her from getting back into the apartment. He wouldn't think twice about locking her out or changing the locks, she decided darkly as she pushed open the door to the apartment's main living room and realised that although she hadn't seen it last night there was actually a huge private terraced area beyond the floor-to-ceiling glass windows of the living room.

Fresh air. Eagerly she made her way towards them.

Tariq glanced at the plain gold watch strapped to his wrist, his mouth compressing. What motivated a woman like Gwynneth Talbot? Didn't she ever think about the danger she was risking when she gave herself to his sex? Or was danger part of the allure? Did she crave the hedonistic excitement her sexual encounters brought her? Didn't she care about the dark, seedy underbelly of the life she was living? Didn't it ever occur to her that she could end up physically harmed or even dead?

She was not his responsibility, he reminded himself angrily as he strode across the floor of the spacious living room after her. He owed her nothing. She meant nothing to him.

It was now dark outside, and unfamiliar scents filled the warm night air. The tantalising smell of food for one, making Gwynneth's stomach growl with hunger. What on earth had she got herself into? She, of all people, who normally lived her life so carefully and cautiously…

'So you're out here, are you?'

She turned round very carefully. The sensation prickling across her skin was arousing emotions that even she could recognise were dangerous. Apprehension, anger, hostility: they might be expected and acceptable, but that hot flare of excitement coupled with that searing mental flashback to last night was very definitely not! Caution urged her to ignore him, go straight to the study and lock herself back inside it. But, inexplicably, she was ignoring caution in favour of something far more confrontational and reckless.

'I needed some fresh air,' she told him pointedly. 'And I—'

Tariq interrupted her, demanding angrily, 'What is it that makes you take such risks? Have you any idea of the danger you could have been in?'

Of all the male moves she had ever experienced, this one had to take the prize. How dared he try to cloak his own behaviour in some kind of faked concern for her?

'Like you'd care!' she scoffed cynically. 'Or was that what you were doing last night—showing me your caring side?'

'My concern last night was directed towards the rather more personal issue of good sexual health,' he told her frankly. 'Something I should have thought would also be of primary importance to a woman of your obvious experience. Didn't last night teach you anything?' he added harshly. 'Or does the danger of what you're doing excite you in some perverted way?'

His anger ignited her own temper, pushing her over the limit of her own self-control. 'For your information, what happened last night isn't something— I'd never— Look, last night was a mistake, all right? It shouldn't have happened but it did. Not that it's any of your business. I don't have to explain myself to you, and I don't care what interpretation you choose to put on what I say or do.'

'No?' he challenged her.

'No,' Gwynneth asserted, and believed that she meant it.

'But you obviously *do* care that your behaviour last night led me to believe that you are a woman who is prepared to have sex with a stranger—and obviously not for the first time.'

Not for the first time? She was tired, she was hungry, and she was still in shock from everything she had experienced. In short, she had endured more than enough! 'Well, that's where you're wrong,' Gwynneth contradicted him angrily.

'And, what's more, last night wasn't only the first time, it was also the last time! I'd rather remain celibate for the rest of my life than—' Dammit, dammit, *dammit*. She was *not* going to cry in front of him! 'Than be subjected to the…the humiliation you forced on me last night!' It was as though his words had applied such unbearable pressure to the place inside her heart that hurt—very badly that she just wasn't able to stop herself from reacting to the pain.

How right she had been to repress her sexuality; how much she wished she had continued to do so. And how very, very much she wished she had never met *him*!

'*Celibate?* A woman like you?'

His contemptuous disbelief burned away what was left of her restraint.

'A woman like me? You mean that because I'm a virgin my sexual curiosity will drive me to sex? After last night?' She shook her head and laughed mirthlessly. 'I promise you, that was experience enough for me to know that celibacy is what I want.'

'*You*—a virgin?' Tariq shook his head incredulously. 'You're lying!' His rebuttal of her words was as emotionally charged as her own rejection of his accusation.

'No, I'm not lying,' Gwynneth said wearily. 'But I can see that you have a vested interest in refusing to believe me. Believe what you like. I don't care.' Her fierce inner emotional conflagration had burned itself out, leaving her feeling drained and vulnerably close to tears, unable to understand why she had made such an intimate disclosure to him.

She had to get away from him before he destabilised her emotional balance even more. Without waiting for him to say anything, she turned away from him and hurried back inside, automatically heading for the protection of the small study and its lock.

Her heart was pounding and she felt wretchedly over-wrought and upset as she leaned against the door and closed her eyes. How had he done this to her normal emotional stability and balance? The stability and balance she had dedicated her life to providing for herself?

Tariq was alone on the large balcony terrace.

A soft breeze whispered restlessly around him. The same breeze which would once surely have whispered against the wondrous hanging gardens of the Hidden Valley. It smelled of the desert and its purity, its freedom. Its sheer vastness and unrelenting harshness forced a man who chose to ignore the dangers inherent in making it his home to accept that he would always have to fight to master it. In the desert there was no mental energy to spare for the self-indulgence of personal feelings. There a man had to put the safety of those who depended on him first or risk extinction; there a man had to create beauty out of its harshness through dedication and vision and most of all by belief in himself, just as his ancestors had done in creating the gardens he was now seeking to restore to their original glory.

She had lied, of course, when she had said that she was a virgin.

But what if she hadn't? What if she was? The desert code was a strict code, a code that protected male honour and female virtue. A code that said an eye for an eye, like for like, and the only way a woman's stolen virtue could be restored to her was via marriage to her despoiler.

But she was *not* a virgin, and he had *not* despoiled her. The walls of the apartment and the building it was in enclosed him, just as marriage would enclose him—like a form of imprisonment. Marriage without love was like bread without salt, and he had no intention of allowing himself to fall in love. That was what his parents had done—or so they had believed.

Had she any idea how vulnerable she was? Didn't she realise how easy it would be for a man in his position, who lacked his scruples, to use her in the most primitive and abusive of ways before abandoning her? She could be kept here in an apartment like this one and not be allowed to leave. She could be forced to accept whatever intimacies a powerful man might choose to enforce on her, and no one would be the wiser until it was too late. She needed to be protected against herself as well as against those men who might abuse her. Didn't she realise the effect her claim to virginity could have on such men? How it would increase their lust for her rather than their respect?

Didn't he, though, have far more important things to worry about than a foolish woman?

CHAPTER SIX

SHE should have claimed the main bedroom and left him to have to sleep in here, Gwynneth thought as she looked at the small sofa pushed against the wall of the second-bedroom-cum-office. Obviously it was a sofabed, but there simply wasn't enough floor space to open it up.

She felt both emotionally and physically exhausted, and yet she still wasn't in the right frame of mind to sleep.

What was it about some people—people like her—that excluded them from the kind of childhood observation of adult love that would make it something to welcome rather than fear for themselves? If all human beings were hardwired to experience emotional love, then why had nature so cruelly decided that some would only ever experience it negatively? In a better world, surely every human being would live within the comfort of a loving relationship all of their lives. Perhaps adopting the 'love thyself' rationale of an egotist was the best way to experience love. But seeing all those other people at the airport in couples had made her painfully aware of the emotional emptiness of her own life. Was that why she had responded so hungrily to Tariq? Had some part of her wanted to play the alchemist and turn the base metal of sexual lust into emotional gold?

Now she was being ridiculous.

She went over to the bookshelves and removed the book on the history of Zuran she had noticed earlier, settling herself as comfortably as she could on the sofa and opening it. To her own surprise, within a very short space of time she had become deeply engrossed in it.

Tariq paused outside the door to the study. There was no sound from inside the room. It was almost midnight. He had eaten the meal he had had sent up, and the young waiter who had brought it from the restaurant had returned to remove his empty plate, along with the untouched meal he had felt morally obliged to order for Gwynneth. He might resent her presence in the apartment but he could hardly let her starve. However, if she wanted to deprive herself of food then that was her choice.

His fingers curled round the door handle. It turned easily in his grip.

A reading lamp illuminated the scene inside the room. Gwynneth was half lying, half sitting on the sofa, deeply asleep, the book she had obviously been reading on the floor. She looked cramped and uncomfortable. She hadn't even bothered to open up the small sofabed.

He turned back towards the door, and then stopped. If she continued to sleep like that she would wake up with a stiff neck, and surely with pins and needles in the foot she had tucked up beneath herself. In her sleep she looked young and oddly vulnerable, her dark lashes feathering shadows against the peach-soft flesh of her face.

Leaving the door open, he walked back over and stood

looking down at her. He was willing her to wake up, to save him the bother of a task he didn't want to perform, but she obviously wasn't going to oblige him. But then why had he expected that she might, in view of the acrimony that existed between them? Even in her sleep she was challenging him.

There was no real need for him to do this, Tariq told himself as he bent to lift her bodily into his arms. In fact, if he left her here the uncomfortable night she would undoubtedly endure might push her into leaving.

Her feet, he noticed, were small and slender, her instep delicately arched, her toenails painted a soft shade of pink.

Determinedly he focused on the open door instead of on her.

She made a small sound and nestled closer to him, her eyes still closed but her lips curling into a soft smile.

The king-sized bed in the main bedroom was large enough to sleep a whole family, never mind two adults, one of whom was fully dressed. And, that being the case, there was no reason why for tonight two adults should not share it, and be able to sleep in it as apart as though they were in separate beds—was there? Not from his point of view, Tariq assured himself. But as he pulled back the covers and placed Gwynneth on the bed his body's urgent response to losing the sensation of having her near made him curse inwardly as he tugged the covers up over her. He looked at the empty half of the bed and exhaled impatiently, before leaving the bedroom and heading back to his study.

There was work he needed to do, he told himself. That was why he had come in here Not because he couldn't trust himself to share the master bed with Gwynneth Talbot without giving in to his body's demand for her closeness.

* * *

Gwynneth studied the note in front of her on the kitchen worktop.

I have some business matters to attend to this morning, but I shall be returning. Tariq.

Tariq. So that was his name. Tariq. She tested it, tasting it and rolling it around her mouth until she was familiar with the shape and feel of it, as though it were his flesh she was sampling and allowing to pleasure her tastebuds.

What time exactly did later in the day mean? she wondered as she smoothed the paper with her fingertip, unconsciously lingering over the strong strokes with which he had written his name. It was almost as though the potent strength of his personality reached out to challenge her via his signature. Her brain tried and failed to rationalise or analyse the complexity of what she was feeling.

The facts—stick to the facts, she warned herself. Facts, unlike feelings and desires, could be firmly pinned down where they belonged.

It had been a shock to wake up this morning and find that she was lying fully dressed in bed, knowing that only one person could have put her there. *The* bed, the one she had slept in with *him* the night before that. Why had he done that? Why had he come for her and, having found her, carried her off to his own room? Had he done it because…? Because what? Because he wanted her but hadn't wanted to wake her up? Get real, she advised herself unsympathetically. She might be fantasising about a repeat performance of last night but that didn't mean that he was.

Fantasising…repeat performance? No way! Even though she was on her own she shook her head in denial, as vigorously as though the trenchant comment came from an alter ego that had a physical presence.

Desperate to distance herself from her unwanted thoughts, she opened the fridge and removed a yoghurt and some fresh fruit.

Outside the sky was a clear, hot blue, and the temptation to have breakfast on the balcony was too much for her to resist.

The warm air smelled faintly of incense and salt. Down below her she could see the hotels, and beyond them the marina and the beach.

Up here she had both the freedom to see what was happening and the privacy not to be seen herself. The warmth of the sun felt wonderful against her English-wintered skin, and had she been here on her own she might have been tempted to slip out of her clothes and bask in its delicious heat, safe in the knowledge that no one could see her. But she wasn't here on her own. And the last thing she wanted was for Tariq to come back and find her sunbathing in the nude.

Since she had come to Zuran on business, not expecting to stay for more than a couple of days, she hadn't brought any kind of resort wear with her—not that she saw herself as the kind of person who would ever want 'resort wear'. The words brought her a mental picture of a weirdly hybrid female—a cross between an aging fifties prom queen in diamonds and layers of chiffon, and a C-list celeb in pink sparkly matching everything, including cowboy boots, hat and tattoo. No, that wasn't her, she thought with a smile. Still, the reality was that if she stayed here much longer she was going to need a couple of clean T-shirts and some underwear.

She peeled back the top from her yoghurt and dipped her spoon into it, balancing the book on Zuran on the table in front of her so that she could continue to read it. She had retrieved it from Tariq's study earlier. She definitely hadn't wanted to go in there for any other reason than to get the book, she reminded herself. And anyway, it had been impossible to tell from its neatness if Tariq had spent the night in there, leaving her to sleep alone.

An hour later she was still reading, totally engrossed in the story of how Zuran had long ago been created out of empty desert by the family who still ruled here. The aim of the current Ruler was, it seemed, to turn Zuran into a good old-fashioned earthly paradise, open to visitors of every culture and colour. By the time Zuran's oil revenues had dwindled from their current gush to a mere trickle it was planned that the country would be *the* favoured and favourite destination of the world's holidaymakers and sports fans.

The book quoted an interview in which the Ruler acknowledged that he was taking a calculated gamble in investing so many billions in developing the small country in such a way. As a financial analyst, Gwynneth could easily imagine the damage that would be done to this plan if the double selling of property to overseas buyers became an open scandal.

A whole chapter of the book was devoted to explaining local customs, and some of the differences between Eastern and Western mindsets. Gwynneth frowned as she read that in the Middle East the giving and accepting of gifts to smooth the way for a variety of negotiations was considered the accepted norm, rather than being labelled detrimentally as bribery, as it would be in Western cultures. The author of the book advised would-be Western businessmen to employ the services of someone experienced in the way business was conducted in Zuran, so as not to cause any loss of face to themselves or others.

It would be far easier—and not merely financially—for Tariq to employ bribery to gain legal ownership of the apartment than it would for her. She had neither money nor contacts; he, she suspected, would have both.

She was about to close the book when she noticed a chapter entitled 'The Hidden Valley'. Her curiosity aroused, she turned to it.

The valley, Gwynneth learned, had originally been a place of great strategic importance, controlling and guarding a camel train route from Zuran into the lands that lay beyond it. According to legend, the valley had been gifted to the son of a favoured concubine by a long-ago Sultan. This son had fortified the valley and built within it a magnificent palace, funding the work with the money he charged travellers to pass through it and use the waters of its oasis. This was said to be replenished by a fast-flowing underground river that ran so far beneath the surface of the sand that no one had ever been able to find it.

It was the water from this river that had enabled the fabled and lost Hanging Gardens of Mjenat to flourish, until a terrible sandstorm—caused, so the story went, by the magic of a jealous rival—destroyed and obliterated the once beautiful gardens, reducing the tiered steps filled with luscious fruits and tropical plants to a series of sand-filled stone ledges where nothing could grow.

Current investigations taking place in the valley seemed to point to the fact that the gardens might actually have existed, the author continued, but they could proceed only very slowly, to minimise any risk to the existing environment. Additionally, the small oasis was definitely fed by an underground spring whose source had yet to be confirmed. Space satellites showed quite clearly where rivers might once have existed in the desert, and where indeed they might continue to exist deep down under the surface.

The current owner of this small, unique place was related to the Zurani royal family, and a prince in his own right. He was apparently dedicating his time and part of his wealth to researching the truth about the past history of his inheritance.

The whole project fascinated her—from its historical, almost fairy-tale past to its modern archaeological present—and she wanted to know more. And not just about the valley. There was something about the prince himself, and the paucity of information about him, that piqued her interest. A modern man who was part of past legend. How did he manage two such opposing parts of himself? Presumably far better than she managed the opposing parts of *herself*, although they were hardly the same. What she had read about him intrigued her. But it did not inflame her in the way that Tariq's dangerously charismatic personality did.

She put the book down, still open at the chapter on the Hidden Valley, and lay back in her chair with her eyes closed. And that was how Tariq found her several minutes later, when he walked sure-footedly and silently towards her.

He hadn't had a good morning. He had gone to the Palace to see the Ruler and the Chief of Police, who had advised them both that, thanks to Tariq's work, the police thought they had now discovered the identity of the Zurani official who was working for the gang. Unfortunately, he'd added, the situation was rather more complicated than they might have hoped.

'Why?' Tariq had asked baldly.

'The man we believe to be working for Chad Rheinvelt is Omar bin Saud al Javir. As you doubtless know, he is related to the traitor Prince Nazir, whose plot to murder the Ruler was thankfully thwarted.'

'This is a very serious accusation,' the Ruler intervened. 'When Prince Nazir and his family were exiled from Zuran, some members of his family disassociated themselves from him and begged for my clemency. Omar's father was one of them.'

'And this is how Omar repays your kindness,' Tariq said curtly.

'From the enquiries we have made we have discovered that the young man in question has given his family many causes to feel ashamed of him. He was dismissed from the University of Zuran for misbehaviour and poor grades. Without his family connections it is doubtful that he would have been given the responsible job he now holds. According to his superior he is a quarrelsome young man with a chip on his shoulder. However, this superior also told me that in recent months Omar had started to behave far more circumspectly, and has been showing a much greater interest in his work.'

'Presumably because Chad has been paying him to work for *him*!' Tariq put in grimly.

'Naturally it is impossible to do anything until we have positive concrete evidence of what is going on,' the Chief of Police continued. 'And for that reason I have now given instructions that Omar's every movement is to be closely watched. If all goes according to plan, we hope to have the evidence we need within the next twenty-four hours. Then we can take him into custody. However, until that happens, and until we have dealt with Chad Rheinvelt and his minions, I would ask, Highness—' the Chief of Police bowed in Tariq's direction '—that you would graciously consent to continuing to give us your assistance. It won't be for too much longer.'

'Keep me informed,' Tariq had instructed him just before he left. 'I want to know the moment anything changes.'

Then, the Chief of Police's request hadn't seemed too much to ask.

Right now, though, here in the apartment even a very few minutes felt dangerously like too much exposure to the growing problem of his reaction to his unwanted house guest.

Gwynneth wasn't just the cause of his lack of sleep last night, she was also the cause of the thoughts and needs that were currently tormenting him.

Gwynneth hadn't heard him come out onto the balcony. But when she opened her eyes the physical effect his presence had on her was so intimate and so disturbing that it shocked her. Her pulse was racing, and she could feel a warm flush rising from her breasts up over her throat. She realised how much she wanted to see him smile at her with warmth and delight.

Delight? Was she going completely mad? She had to put some distance between them, and fast.

He was blocking her path to the French doors, but she was too uncomfortably aware of her own unwanted reaction to him to let that stop her. She leapt up and, still holding the book tightly in her arms, made to push past him, gasping aloud when instead of moving he grabbed hold of her, his hands gripping the tender flesh of her upper arms so hard it felt as though he could break her bones if he chose to do so. It seemed as if he too realised that, and his grip slackened—not enough for her to be able to break free, but enough so that he could almost absently rhythmically rub her flesh with the pads of his thumbs, as though he was trying to smooth away any pain he might have caused.

'Let go of me,' she demanded, with more bravado than she was actually feeling. There was something very sensually disturbing and primitive about that rhythmic touch, and the answering surge it caused within her. As though something very dark and hidden deep inside her was responding to the rhythm he had set, just as it had done that first night when…

Her faced burned even more hotly as she realised where her thoughts were taking her and the trap that was waiting for her there. She wanted to close her eyes to blot him out, but she was afraid to do so in case that sensual pulse he was calling up took her over.

'Why?' The smile he gave her was knowing and unkind. As though to underline what he meant, he brushed the backs of his fingers down her bare arm.

Her body's reaction was immediate—and very physical. So much so that before she could stop herself she looked betrayingly down her at her breasts. Her nipples, clearly outlined and flauntingly erect, swelled eagerly against the fabric of her top.

Like someone in a trance she watched as he lifted his hand and brushed his knuckles very slowly over one nipple. Her breath jerked out of her body, visibly and audibly. She couldn't even use the retaliatory visual weapon of looking at his crotch. That all-encompassing immaculate white robe hid anything and everything there might have been to see. But her gaze had dropped to his body and his followed it, pinning it there whilst she tried to escape, as uselessly as a small bird trapped in honey.

'Wanton,' she heard him taunt her. 'You devour me with your eyes. Just as you—'

'No!' Gwynneth denied wildly, trying to pull away, forgetting that he was still holding her, shocked to discover that she was being yanked back into his possession, into his arms, his body, whilst his mouth covered hers, smothering its rebellion and stealing her will to fight.

What was this? Why was it happening? Her thoughts spilled dizzily into space, escaping her as fast as she tried to catch them, whilst inside her a whole new universe of sensation and need exploded in a shower of meteorites, blinding and dazzling her.

She could feel the engine of his heartbeat driving her own, as though it were pushing the blood through her veins, as though without it—without him—there could be no life for her. Behind the darkness of her closed eyes she felt the infinity of limitless aching need. His tongue prised apart her lips like a conqueror, and then dipped triumphantly into her mouth's sweetness. His hand enclosed her breast and her pulse seemed to stop beating before racing unsteadily in fierce excitement. The book slipped from her hold and onto the floor. The noise shocked through her.

Immediately Tariq released her.

'Why did you have to do that?'

The anguish he could hear in her voice hardened Tariq's mouth. She might not be the professional call girl he had first assumed, but neither was she the victim she was now trying to appear—and they both knew it.

'Why?' he answered mockingly. 'Because you let me.'

'I *let* you? That's what men like you always tell yourselves when you have to force yourself on a woman, when you make her give you something she doesn't want to, isn't it?' Gwynneth demanded bitterly. 'Well, if you're hoping to…to sexually harass me into leaving this apartment so that you can claim it, you're wasting your time.'

He was frowning at her, his mouth compressing with anger.

'Me? Sexually harass you? If that's true, then what was the

way you looked at my body all about? How exactly do you explain that?'

'I wasn't looking at your body,' Gwynneth insisted, but she knew the guilty colour darkening her face was giving her away.

'Liar. You looked at me to see if I was aroused.'

'And were you?'

Gwynneth blinked, as though she couldn't believe what she had just heard herself say—which she couldn't. She lifted her hand to her forehead, wondering grimly if some unseen and malevolently inclined genie had got out of his bottle and into her vocal cords.

Tariq looked at her sharply, thinking that she was being facetious. She must know that he had been aroused, otherwise he would never have done what he just had. But her expression told him quite plainly that she did not.

'I've got far more important things to do with my time than waste it on this kind of rubbish,' he told her flatly. That much at least was true. But it wasn't true that he wasn't thinking about her, despite the other calls on his time. He couldn't stop doing so. And not just thinking…

CHAPTER SEVEN

ANOTHER night spent sleeping in that huge bed, waking what felt like every few minutes just to check that she was still alone, her heart overdosing on adrenaline.

With fear, because she was afraid that Tariq might come to her, *for* her, sliding into the big bed beside her to take her in his arms and make her his?

Or with guilty excitement, because it was what she longed for him to do?

He drew her physically and emotionally as no other man had ever done, and fighting against the effect he was having on her had Gwynneth on a constant seesaw of thoughts and feelings.

Even when she closed her eyes and tried to sleep she couldn't get away from him, because her senses immediately assaulted her defences with sensually erotic images of their bodies entwined together, his hand resting possessively on her breast, playing with her eagerly erect nipple, then sliding teasingly down her body to push her legs open so that he could explore and enjoy her body and its response to him. And it wanted to respond to him so much.

How could she want him so badly? A man who…

A man who made her want to ask him a thousand questions

about himself. About what he was and how he had become that; how he had grown up; how he lived; how he thought and felt; what his dreams were, and his nightmares too.

And that wasn't just wanting him physically. That was... Not love, she denied in panic, thrusting the thought away from her. It couldn't be love. Or at least not love as she had always imagined it to be. Love came from knowing a person; it meant trusting them and feeling safe with them. She didn't know Tariq, she didn't trust him, and she certainly didn't feel safe with him.

And yet he had given her nothing to fear. As the bed evidenced, she had slept alone in it last night. Could it be truer to say that she did not *want* to feel safe with him, that she enjoyed that exciting frisson of fear the thought of him touching her gave her? Maybe she didn't really want to trust him either. It was a long time since she had fully trusted anyone and she had grown used to refusing to do so. Trusting someone meant allowing herself to be vulnerable to them, letting them into the inner sanctum of her most private emotional places—places she had kept guarded for so long...

It was time she got up, instead of allowing her thoughts to roam such dangerous byways.

'You are to be congratulated on such a speedy conclusion to what might have been a most unpleasant business.' The Ruler smiled approvingly at the Chief of Police, who had just announced to both his master and Tariq that Omar was now in prison, having admitted his involvement with the gang, and that all the members of the gang, including Chad Rheinvelt, had been apprehended and would be facing either trial or deportation.

'Unfortunately, we do still have one area of concern,' the Chief of Police admitted.

'Which is?' Tariq asked.

'We arrested Omar in the early hours of this morning, as he left a meeting with Rheinvelt. Later, when he was questioned, he told us that Rheinvelt had been asking him about Prince Tariq. It seems the gang leader was suspicious of His Highness's reasons for agreeing to assist him. Omar told Rheinvelt that in his opinion there was no way His Highness would ever do anything that might harm the Ruler or his family, and that far from needing money, as Rheinvelt apparently believed, His Highness is an extremely wealthy man. Omar further claimed that Rheinvelt swore to punish His Highness for deceiving him, and that he heard Rheinvelt giving instructions to this effect.'

'What exactly are you trying to say?' Tariq demanded. 'The gang is under lock and key.'

'Yes, but Rheinvelt has many contacts, not all of whom were visibly attached to this gang. He is a man who does not trust anyone. We have questioned him, of course, but he is an old hand at this sort of thing and has told us nothing. However, Omar remains adamant that Rheinvelt has put out a contract on His Highness—and on the somewhat softer targets, perhaps, of those close to him,' the Chief announced portentously. 'Naturally we are treating this threat very seriously, and if it does exist, then we shall discover the identity and whereabouts of his hitman. But until we do I have to warn His Highness to be on guard. We will provide bodyguards.'

Tariq shook his head in immediate refusal.

'That is not the way I have lived my life, nor is it the way I intend to live it,' he informed the Chief coolly.

'I would counsel you to think again, Highness,' the Chief of Police urged him, adding meaningfully, 'Please recall, your intimate friends could also be vulnerable to such an attack.'

Tariq frowned heavily at the policeman's words and told him curtly, 'They cannot possibly get close enough to the Ruler to harm him or his family.'

'It is not the Greatest amongst the Great of whom I am thinking,' was the Chief of Police's deliberately emphasised reply.

'Then to whom *are* you referring?' Tariq demanded impatiently. The Ruler was, after all, his closest relative.

The Chief of Police salaamed and informed him apologetically, 'Highness, because of the risks involved in this affair, I appointed men to keep a watch over the apartment block at Al Mirahmi. A young woman has been seen to leave and enter His Highness's apartment on a number of separate occasions. I beg forgiveness for this intrusion,' he added hastily, 'but His Highness will understand that his position within the family of our esteemed Ruler—may Allah protect him—has necessitated this.'

There were a good many more heavily embellished courtly effusions, but in the end it all boiled down to one thing. Gwynneth had been seen leaving and entering his apartment. In the eyes of the Chief of Police, and therefore very possibly in the eyes of anyone else who had seen her, she was his, and therefore potentially at risk should it turn out that Omar's information was correct.

This was how men of his country thought. Even if he attempted to explain the tangle of circumstances which had led to Gwynneth occupying the apartment at the same time as he was doing so, knowing what he did, the Chief of Police would still not be totally convinced. And neither, Tariq suspected, would Chad. Tariq had refused the offer of a prostitute; Tariq had a woman living with him; that woman must be important enough to him for any harm done there to serve as a warning to him. That was how men like Chad thought, and it was as pointless trying to change his thinking as it was trying to change that of his own countrymen.

'She, of course, is a more vulnerable target for them. It may even be that they will attempt to kill her as a warning to you,' the Chief of Police murmured almost apologetically, plainly sensing Tariq's anger.

This was exactly what he had just thought himself. And Tariq had to admit that the scenario the Chief of Police was outlining to him was all too feasible. Which meant...

Which meant that for her own safety Ms Gwynneth Talbot had to be packed off back to her own country and her own life just as quickly as possible. Quickly, discreetly, efficiently. Without any kind of fuss or delay. In a manner that would brook no opposition from Ms Gwynneth Talbot herself and that would not oblige him to tell her the truth. The thought of such a money-hungry young woman being free to approach a British journalist with her story, and the scale of potential damage to Zuran's future success as a safe tourist destination, was more than enough to convince him of that. Some plan would have to be made to get her to leave without arousing her suspicions, and Tariq decided he knew just the right one.

This time he made his way back to the apartment which thankfully he would soon be able to quit via his own chauffeur-driven limousine. But he still had his driver drop him off out of view of any of the windows of the apartment.

He found Gwynneth on the terrace, once again reading one of his books. This time one on local customs.

As always when he saw her afresh after any kind of absence from her, he had to struggle to control the sudden upsurge in his heartbeat and his desire to go to her and take hold of her.

The sooner she was back in her own country, the better, he decided grimly, as he glanced briefly at her and then looked away.

Gwynneth watched him in smouldering silence. The apartment had felt so empty without him, and she hated it that he could make her feel like that.

'I've been thinking about your situation with regard to this apartment,' Tariq announced without any preamble.

'*My* situation?' Gwynneth challenged him pointedly. Where the apartment was concerned, and with it Teresa and baby Anthony's future, she wasn't going to let him get away with anything—not one tiny little thing.

Tariq shrugged. 'As I understand it, if you are found to be the legal owner of this apartment it is your intention to return to your home and put it on the market—isn't that so?'

Cautiously Gwynneth nodded her head.

'In order to short-circuit what could very probably be a long-drawn-out and complex set of procedures, I am prepared to offer you the full market price of the apartment. By tomorrow night you can be home in Britain.'

He was *what*? Had she heard him correctly?

'*You* want to buy the apartment—from *me*?' she asked him, spacing out the words slowly and carefully, as though she wasn't sure of their validity.

'That's right.'

Gwynneth stared at him suspiciously. Why was he suggesting this? She didn't believe for one minute that it was out of any desire to help her—far from it.

'Why would you want to do that?' she challenged him.

'I don't have the time to waste on haggling and bartering over this.'

Gwynneth's eyebrows rose in patent disbelief. 'But I thought that haggling and bartering was the bedrock of Middle Eastern business methods,' she told him sweetly.

Tariq was looking at her as though he itched to put his hands round her neck and shake her into submission. 'I am simply trying to help you,' he told her unconvincingly.

Gwynneth put on a coolly disbelieving look. 'Yeah—as if,' she responded inelegantly, and shot him a feral smile. She was enjoying riling him and getting under his skin so much that she must possess a rogue love-of-danger gene she hadn't hitherto known about, she decided, as she waited to see what his next move would be. At least this was keeping a safe distance between them physically, and helping her to erect crash barriers against him inside her head.

Her head—but what about her heart?

What about it? It didn't come into this equation and she wasn't going to let it.

'You don't fool me. You're trying to sell me this deal like it's in my interests and to my benefit. But no way am I going to fall for that. You've got some kind of personal agenda going on here that makes ownership of this apartment in a hurry something you want,' she challenged him.

The look on his face told her there was something important she had neglected to factor in. Talk about thunder clouds rolling down from on high—never mind the lightning glittering in those mercury-grey eyes! One direct hit from that and her will-power could well be history.

'Maybe what I want "in a hurry" is you out of my life,' he retorted savagely.

Gwynneth winced. She should have been expecting that.

'The market price of the apartment is three-quarters of a million pounds sterling. I am prepared to write you a cheque for one million pounds right now—that will cover your costs as well.'

The real market value of the apartment was closer to £500,000, but Tariq didn't want to waste valuable time arguing. He wanted her gone—and not just for her own sake. She was beginning to affect him too much and too often, and that wasn't something he intended to allow to continue.

'A cheque?' Gwynneth questioned suspiciously. Was he somehow trying to cheat her out of the apartment? Did he really think she was that much of a fool to fall for something like that? And besides, she already knew, because the young official had told her, that the apartment was worth in the region of £500,000. So why was Tariq offering her so much more? Because he thought her greed would make her jump to accept his offer? Which meant that he had to have an ulterior motive. But what? It could be that his offer was quite simply a scam. Or perhaps, whatever his reason for wanting the apartment, it had nothing to do with money.

What should she do? Her first duty was to Teresa and Anthony, and she owed it to them to get the highest price she could for the apartment. Perhaps she could shock Tariq into telling her a bit more by letting him know that she wasn't as easily deceived as he seemed to think.

Taking a deep breath, she asked him derisively, 'Do you really think I'm that much of a fool?'

'What do you mean?' There was a very ominous and warning note in his voice, but Gwynneth chose to ignore it.

'Isn't it obvious?' she said mock-sweetly. 'You give me a

cheque, I sign over the apartment, and then I find that your cheque can't be honoured.'

'*What?* You're accusing me of dishonesty?' he demanded in disbelief.

Gwynneth lifted her chin determinedly.

'You obviously want the apartment very badly, and common sense tells me that you must have an ulterior motive. On the face of it, you've offered me far more than the apartment is actually worth. Why would you do that? As an act of charity?' She gave him a thin smile and shook her head. 'I don't think so. Perhaps you expected me to be so eager to accept your offer that I wouldn't stop to question why you were making it. Perhaps you hoped to defraud me via a dud cheque—or perhaps you know something about the apartment that I don't know which increases its value. There has to be a reason that benefits you.' She gave a small shrug. 'Why else would you want it?'

'Is that how you assess everything?' Tariq asked her with open contempt. 'In terms of financial value?'

He was treating *her* with contempt? Surely it should be the other way around? Somehow he had wrongfooted her, Gwynneth knew, but she was not sure how. With the sleight of hand of some souk *fakir* switching tumblers and dice, he had managed to transform her moral superiority into his own, and make her look cheap and avaricious.

'This is a financial deal, and the apartment is a financial asset and must be valued as such,' she answered as firmly as she could. 'I can't and won't agree to your proposition until I have had it independently valued.'

'You *dare* to question my word?'

Gwynneth stood her ground.

'Yes, I do.'

She heard him mutter something under his breath which she suspected was not complimentary, and then he was striding towards her, reaching for her wrists and manacling them within the hard grip of his strong fingers.

'Get your hands off me!' Gwynneth demanded sharply, trying to pull herself free.

Tariq had simply intended to vent his fury by shaking her, but the moment she fought to break free of his hold his reasons for imprisoning her and the warning he had given himself earlier were forgotten, swamped by a surge of primitive male desire. He pulled her against his body, pinning her wrists behind her back and keeping them there in one swift movement that left her almost speechless—and seething.

'Let go of me!' she demanded through gritted teeth. But then she made the mistake of looking up at his mouth, and found that she couldn't stop looking. Now the liquid heat pouring through her veins wasn't just anger. Maybe it wasn't *even* anger. Maybe it was…

She heard him mutter something, and then he bent his head. She heard herself moan as the force of his kiss tipped her head back and he lifted one hand from her pinioned wrists to support the back of her neck, his fingers splaying into her hair. This time she didn't need to question whether or not he was aroused. She knew he was. She could feel the hot, hard pulse of his erection pressing into the softness of her own flesh.

Behind her closed eyelids a thousand and one erotic images tormented her. A thousand and one sensual intimacies spread out over a lifetime of dark starlit nights in a land where heaven and earth touched, where the desert met the sky, and where a woman touched that heaven in the arms of her lover. In that place they would share together the transforming wonder that was human passion and human desire and human love…

Frantically Gwynneth pulled her mouth from beneath Tariq's. What was happening to her was beginning to scare her—and badly.

Tariq could feel her heart thudding into his with quick fast beats like that of a trapped bird. He put his hand over it, watching the way her expression changed and her breath caught in her throat as though on a ratchet whilst her heart-beat almost doubled.

What was it about this pale-skinned, turbulent, impossible woman that pushed him beyond the boundaries of the self-control he had thought unbreachable? Inside his head, thoughts he hadn't known he could have jostled against one another, their sharp edges raking his pride, leaving it raw with open wounds. He took a deep breath, his chest lifting power-fully, and then shook his head, as though trying to shake off the unwanted reality of his thoughts. A heat like that of the desert sand under the midday sun seared through his body. There was no escape from it, or from the place it was taking him. The only release for him, the only place he could slake the thirst of his desire, was within her. Like an oasis in the desert, she lured and drew him to her.

In another age he would have summoned a Wise One to remove the spell she had surely put on him—but it was a spell which his senses told him had possessed her as well.

The frantic beat of her heart beneath his hand told him how much she wanted him, and his own reaction to it betrayed how much he wanted her. His desire for her was an insistent driving force that filled his mind and his body and drove his heart-beat. It was his life force, and without it he would die.

He lifted his hand to her breast, soft and round, filling his palm. He drew his fingertips to her nipple, tugging sensually on it whilst she shuddered against him and cried out with pleasure. Inside his head he could almost see the pale globe of flesh, almost taste its sweetness. His erection stiffened and throbbed painfully.

How could she be letting Tariq do this? How could she *not*? an inner eager voice demanded hungrily. Somehow the simple act of his fingertips playing with her nipple was enforcing a rhythmic urgency on her that had her grinding her lower body into him whilst she pressed her lips to his throat, her tongue-tip tasting the salty sweat on the heat of his skin. She felt him pushing her clothes out of the way, to expose her breasts to the coolness of the air-conditioned room and to the heat of his touch, her own arousal. In the mirror hanging on the adjacent wall she could see the dark splay of his fingers against the pale outline of her breast as she pressed herself into his body. The sight was unbearably erotic, making her shudder tightly in response to its message.

In a far-off century there would have been nothing to stop him from taking this pale-skinned seductress and making her his willing slave, locking her away in the luxury of his harem, where no other male eyes could see her and no other male hands could touch her. Then she would have been his to enjoy, whenever and wherever he wished. But this was now, and he was…he was dangerously, recklessly, unacceptably out of control, Tariq admitted grimly. He forced himself to release her.

He had let her go. So why was she standing here looking at him as though she wanted…? Quickly Gwynneth straightened her clothes, her fingers made clumsy by reluctance and thwarted physical need.

And it was *only* physical need that she felt, she reassured herself fiercely as she stepped back from him and told him jerkily, 'Wrong move! If that was supposed to make me change my mind and agree to sell the apartment to you, it hasn't worked!'

Before he could retaliate, she turned round and almost ran to the main door, yanking it open and slipping through it as he called out to her to stop.

CHAPTER EIGHT

WHAT an idiot she was, coming out without her bag, and with no hat or sunglasses, Gwynneth derided herself as she stood in the hot sunshine and shielded her eyes to look uncertainly back at the apartment building.

She could go back. She *should* go back. But she wasn't going to.

Because she was afraid of what could happen if she did? She was afraid, yes, but not of Tariq. An inner female knowledge she hadn't known she possessed told her that there was no likelihood of Tariq forcing himself on her. Why should he, after all, when they both knew he did not need to? She was so sexually attuned to him and by him that her whole body positively vibrated every time he came anywhere near her. Vibrated? Now, why had that particular word popped into her mind?

If she hadn't felt morally obliged to do what she could financially for Teresa and Anthony, she would have been tempted to simply walk away and leave Tariq in possession of the flat. After all, there were more important things in life than money, and her peace of mind was one of them. Her peace of mind and her self-respect.

Now that she was away from him, and had broken free of

the powerful orbit of his sexuality, she could think more clear-headedly about what had happened to her. The discovery that she had after all inherited her father's sensual nature made her feel a lifetime's worth of conflicting emotions. Anger and fear, resentment and a desire to fight her own need—but once she was in Tariq's arms these had immediately morphed into not so much eager compliance as something far more proactive. It had been a battle of age-old female sexual shame versus a glorious, wild 'I can touch the sky' feeling of power and pleasure. And those were just the emotions she could easily recognise. There was a whole lot more going on underneath that was too scary for her to investigate.

What she felt was like… She stood in the street, screwing up her eyes and wrinkling her nose as she concentrated on finding the perfect metaphor to describe her current state of mind. The closest she could get was to say it was like standing on a bridge looking down into unmoving very deep water, knowing that she was too close to the edge and that for her own safety she needed to move away. But instead of doing so, or even just staying where she was, she was moving forward, daring herself to see how much of a risk she could take. Because secretly she *wanted* to throw herself off that bridge and into that water? Because she *wanted* to take that risk and to feel the exhilaration of that freefall into danger before the water closed over her, dragging her down into its unknown depths?

Up above her in the apartment Tariq watched her. If he went after her and she ran off it would draw the kind of attention he most certainly didn't want to a situation he wanted even less.

What was the matter with him? He was behaving with the kind of recklessness he had always despised in others. He moved back from the window, all too aware of the swollen ache of his erection—something else to despise himself for. To a man who had always considered himself to be more aesthetic than carnal, his body's stubborn refusal to control its lust for a woman his mind wanted to reject was as distasteful as it was infuriating.

He turned away. Her reaction to his offer to buy the apartment from her was still rubbing his pride raw, like tiny grains of sand against skin. What was she up to? Did she think that by holding out she could get him to raise his offer still higher? He could taste the bitterness of his own angry contempt. For her or for himself?

He would have to find some way to bring an end to this increasingly dangerous situation. And it *was* dangerous—and not just because of Chad Rheinvelt, he admitted unwillingly.

One option would be to arrange for her to be told that she did not own the apartment but that she would be fully compensated for its value. Then he could leave everything to be dealt with by the Zurani government department concerned. But that would mean involving others, which in turn would mean talk—or, more relevantly, gossip. About Gwynneth, about him, about their shared nights together under the same roof. All leading to the kind of speculation he abhorred.

A look of grim hardness tightened the bones in his face. That was something he was not prepared to countenance. No way. The Ruler, of course, knew exactly why he had not been able to move out of the apartment prior to the discovery of Omar's identity. But Tariq had his own reasons for not wanting what had been going on to be made public.

He had wasted enough time already on Ms Gwynneth Talbot and the problems she was causing him. It was time they were brought to an end. He had other and far more important calls on his time and his emotions—not least several pre-organised meetings, some here in Zuran, others in the valley itself, with certain specialists to discuss various aspects of his plans for the valley.

With the encouragement of the Ruler he was considering the advantages of making the whole valley a heritage site, endowing it for the benefit of their people, but this was not a project that could be rushed. It was one, though, that was very close to his heart. Other men might leave children behind them to mark their existence; *his* mark upon the face of time would be made in the restoration of the legendary hanging gardens and by turning them into a place of wonder and beauty that could be enjoyed by many rather than kept for the pleasure of a chosen few. That was his dream and his goal.

And a long-legged fair-skinned woman was not going to deflect him from it. He glanced at his watch. If he didn't leave now he was going to be late for today's meeting with the Ruler's own specialist horticulturist, who had already been out to the valley to take some samples of its flora.

Why on earth hadn't she come back? Or was he being naïve? Was this yet another ploy of some kind?

Thank goodness for modern air-conditioned shopping centres, Gwynneth thought with relief, as she hurried out of the sun and into the welcome shaded coolness of the large shopping mall a small distance away from the apartment block. Not that she could do anything other than window shop, since she hadn't brought her bag out with her.

But at least she was away from Tariq.

An hour later, when she or rather her overheated passions

had had time to cool down, she decided that she needed to do everything she could to expedite a speedy decision with regard to ownership of the apartment. Even if that meant camping out in Zuran's land registry offices until she got an answer. But first she would have to go back to the apartment, smarten herself up a bit and get her purse. And that meant…

Don't think about it, she warned herself as she left the shopping mall.

She blinked in the fierce glare of the bright sunlight and paused to shade her eyes before looking to check that the road leading to the hotel was clear and starting to walk across it.

She had only taken a few steps when out of nowhere a car screeched round a corner and came racing towards her, its driver too busy speaking into his mobile to be aware of her. She could see the danger and her own vulnerability, but was too shocked to be able to move. And then suddenly firm hands grabbed hold of her, half dragging and half pushing her out of the path of the car as it swerved violently close to her and then roared off.

The entire incident had taken only a few seconds, but those few seconds could have been her last, Gwynneth realised, and she turned to give her rescuer a grateful smile and stammer her thanks. He was a shortish man, close to middle age, and obviously an Arab although he was wearing European clothes.

'You are all right?' he asked her courteously.

Gwynneth nodded, feeling suddenly shaky. 'When I checked the road there was nothing there.' She didn't want him to think she had just walked out in front of the car. 'And then suddenly the car was there, and the driver didn't see me. He was on the phone…' Her disjointed sentences quavered into the late-afternoon heat. She turned to look in the direction the car had come from as her rescuer guided her across the road.

'Thank you so much—' she began a second time, but he shook his head, turning away from her to disappear into the crowd of people emerging from the shopping mall.

She was still feeling slightly shaky when she reached the apartment block. Despite the coolness of its foyer, her heart was thumping erratically, and a fine film of dewy nervous perspiration was dampening her hairline. But it was the thought of Tariq that was responsible for her anxiety, not her close call with the car.

All the way up in the lift her stomach was churning.

Five minutes later she was standing outside the main door to the apartment. Automatically she put her hand down for her bag and her key card, before remembering that she had left the flat without bothering to pick up her bag. The foyer door was unlocked during the day, so she hadn't remembered till now.

No bag, no key card, no way of getting into the flat. Her shoulders rounded slightly with defeat. There was only one thing she could do now. Taking a heroically deep breath, she pulled herself up to her full height and rang the bell.

The seconds ticked by as she strained to hear some sound of movement inside the apartment.

Perhaps Tariq was asleep. Cue distracting mental image of him in bed, sheet pushed down to his hips, the warm sherry-gold of his skin satin-sleek, not just inviting but compelling her to reach out and touch it…

No! She didn't want *those* kind of thoughts, thank you very much. What would she do if he assumed that her return was an invitation to him to continue where he had left off? Would she have the strength of will to resist him if he picked her up in his arms and carried her into the cool shadows of her bedroom and once there…?

Gwynneth breathed in, and then exhaled gustily. If she was really keen for it not to happen, why exactly was she lingering so lovingly over every small mental detail of a supposedly threatening seduction scenario? Anyone peeking into her mind right now would be forgiven for thinking she was actually building an image of something she *wanted* to happen, not stressing over something she didn't.

Far better instead to imagine him standing in silence in the hallway, enjoying her distress. In silence, naked, a towel wrapped round his lower body... Oh, stop it! she told herself irritably.

Perhaps she should ring the bell one last time. She put her finger on the buzzer and pressed it hard.

Nothing. Nothing and no one. She leaned against the wall, feeling defeated.

Now what was she going to do? She was locked out of the apartment and instead of suggesting solutions her rebellious mind was playing games with her.

'So what is to be done about this young woman who claims ownership of the apartment via her late father?' The Ruler pursed his lips, and then remarked blandly, 'She is of your father's race, I understand?

Tariq's eyes narrowed.

'You are well informed, Greatest amongst the Great.'

The Ruler's plump face creased into a wide smile. Tariq only used this mode of address when he wanted to be sardonic.

'Our excellent Chief of Police, Saulud bin Sharif, felt obliged to give me a full report on the young woman.' His expression became far more serious. 'She must not be exposed to danger, Tariq.'

'She will not be.'

The Ruler waited patiently, but Tariq was plainly not going to say any more about the young woman the Ruler had been told was as beautiful as the morning sunrise.

'Excellent.' He smiled again at his grim-looking young relative who, as a prince in his own right, was seated cross-legged on the divan opposite his own. Tariq's height meant that the Ruler had to crick his neck to look up into his eyes.

A manservant was hovering close by with a coffee pot. Tariq covered his cup with the fluid movement of one long-fingered hand in an automatic gesture of denial, his mouth twitching slightly in disapproval when the Ruler reached for yet another sweetmeat.

'My physician warns me of the dangers of too many sweet things, Tariq, but…' The Ruler gave a small dismissive shrug. *'In Sha' Allah,'* he said, fatalistically.

'Your people need you to lead them into the future, and so do your sons,' Tariq murmured quietly.

The Ruler looked at him, and then put down the sugar-dusted square of Turkish delight he had been about to put in his mouth.

'It is when you make pronouncements such as that that I see your father in you the most, Tariq,' he sighed.

'There is nothing of him in me other than where he has left the physical marks of his fathering on me,' Tariq answered grimly. Somewhere deep inside he still felt the pain turned to bitterness of his father's desertion.

The Ruler shook his head patiently. 'Your father was a highly intelligent and far-seeing man in many ways. He saw what my father had done, and showed me how I could build upon those things. I know he caused your mother and you great pain, and that I cannot condone, but many of the projects I have undertaken sprang from the seeds of his vision. In that

I have much cause to be grateful to him. And much cause as well to be grateful for his bestowal on my household of his son. We should perhaps not blame him too much for not being able to adapt to our ways. Your mother, after all, refused to adapt to his.'

Tariq stared at him. 'He *abandoned* her.'

'He left Zuran alone because your mother refused to leave with him—as she had agreed to do when they married,' the Ruler corrected him quietly. 'They agreed they would live in Zuran for some years, and then in Britain. But when the time came she went back on her word.'

'That is not what she told me.'

'Nevertheless, it is the truth.'

'So why did she not say this to me?'

'Maybe she thought you too young, or perhaps she feared that you might judge her. I know that he would have taken you with him had he not felt that it was best for you that you remain here. He was a man who had the heart of a nomad, a man whose work and nature made it impossible for him to settle long in one place. He left you with your mother out of love for you, Tariq.'

'Why has this not been said to me before—by you if not by my mother?'

'Sometimes awareness must wait upon events,' the Ruler told him sagely, and then he inclined his head and clapped his hands, indicating that their meeting was over.

Tariq got to his feet with fluid ease, salaaming before leaving the room.

CHAPTER NINE

THE RULER had given him much to think about. But a deeper consideration of the unexpected revelations about his father would have to wait until another time. Tariq glanced at his watch and immediately lengthened his stride and increased his speed.

He had assumed, when he had seen Gwynneth standing in the street below the apartment block and frowning, that she had realised that she had left without either a key or any money, and so he had waited for her immediate return.

When she hadn't come back he had toyed with the idea of going out and leaving her to a long, uncomfortable wait for his return, but an inbuilt sense of responsibility had stopped him from taking that kind of retaliatory action. Zuran's temperatures topped forty degrees Centigrade at this time of year; she was British, and fair skinned, and she had gone out without anything to cover her exposed head and delicate skin. He wasn't going to take the risk of her doing something foolish that might result in her suffering from heatstroke or worse because she couldn't get into the apartment.

However, his good intentions had been undermined when he had received a telephone call from one of the Ruler's secretaries, requesting his presence at the palace.

He had planned to keep the meeting as short as he possibly could, but his second cousin's revelations about his own father had hijacked his intentions. It was now over four hours since he had left the apartment.

By the time he reached the doors to the palace used by family members, his car and driver were already there waiting for him, the bodywork of the black Mercedes polished to a dust-free gleam.

A uniformed palace guard opened the door for him and the cool silence of the air-conditioned interior embraced him. The imposing palm-lined dual carriageway that ran from the palace to the city had been modelled after London's Mall, although here the wide grass verges had to be kept green with a complex under-soil watering system, and the colourful formal bedding provided by flowering annuals in London was provided here by a rich array of tropical shrubs and plants. Gilded lamp standards were decorated with mosaic-tiled framed images of the Ruler, and in the distance the gold-leaf dome of a mosque glittered in the sunlight.

His driver turned off the imposing Road of the Ruler into an equally wide but far busier thoroughfare. Beyond the dark-tinted car windows Tariq could see the glass exteriors of the many new office and apartment blocks lining the road. He was a member of the select private conglomerate that was responsible for financing a large proportion of them. Zuran City was booming, but the Ruler and his advisers were keeping its development under firm control.

Up ahead of him he could see the shimmer of the new resort complex, and beyond that the area out in the Gulf where men were working on the final stages of building new hotels and villas on land reclaimed from the sea to create the magnificent Palm Island, its trunk the road connecting it to the shore and each palm leaf a long narrow spur of land complete with water frontage.

Tariq had a financial interest in this venture as well, the profit from which was projected to run into billions of dollars.

But it wasn't his growing wealth that occupied his thoughts as the Mercedes sped along the private lane reserved for use by the Royal Family, and neither was it the unexpectedness of the Ruler's revelations about his late father.

He instructed his driver to drop him off within walking distance of the apartment, oblivious to the eager female interest he was attracting as he slid on a pair of aviator sunglasses and emerged from the Mercedes to stride past the exclusive designer shops either side of the palm-lined street, the robe he had donned for the formality of his meeting billowing slightly in the warm breeze.

Gwynneth had been loath to leave the apartment block a second time without any money, and, given that the Zuran land registry office was too far away for her to walk there, she had decided that she had no alternative other than to wait for Tariq to return and let her into the apartment.

Always providing he did return.

Of course he would.

But what if he didn't?

She had brought back from the shopping mall a free magazine, which she had now read from cover to cover several times. During the course of this inspection she had discovered that an apartment similar to her own was currently on sale for £500,000, confirming all her suspicions. *Why* had Tariq offered her a million pounds to give up her claim to this one?

The hum of the air-conditioning was making her feel drowsy. She sat down on the cool tiled floor and leaned back against the wall. Within minutes she was fast asleep.

Tariq frowned when he got out of the lift and saw her seated on the floor, leaning against the wall. She was asleep, her face pale and her hair tousled. There was a small smudge of shadow along her cheekbone, as though she had rubbed it in distress. There was a bottle of water on the floor beside her, along with a magazine, both bearing the logo of a mall complex. Such items were given free to visitors, and he guessed that she must have been there.

The sight of her disturbed him more than he wanted to admit—and not sexually this time. This time his feelings were far, far more dangerous than merely sexual, because this time they contained both concern for her and a strong desire to protect her—if necessary from herself.

He hunkered down beside her and spoke her name quietly. 'Gwynneth.'

Gwynneth smiled in her sleep in acknowledgement of the familiar voice.

Tariq exhaled and lifted one hand to her face, to steady her in case she slipped, using the other to give her a small shake.

Gwynneth sighed luxuriously and turned her face into his hand, rubbing her cheek against it and making a soft purring sound.

Tariq's fingers bit into her shoulder and abruptly Gwynneth woke up.

Tariq was crouching down on the floor next to her, his eyes on a level with hers. Her own widened, whilst colour burned up under her skin. She tried to look away from him, but her gaze was trapped as helplessly as though his had magnetised it.

'How long have you been here?' he asked curtly.

Gwynneth shook her head. Her muscles felt slightly stiff.

'I don't know. What time is it now?'

Her breath rattled in her lungs as he lifted his wrist and shot back the hem of his sleeve to reveal the tawny, sinewy strength of his wrist. How on earth could such a simple action, the mere sight of a plain watch encircling a man's wrist, have this kind of effect on her?

'Almost six p.m.'

'I came back about three.'

Just over an hour after he had left.

'I hadn't intended to be gone so long. I realised after you'd gone that you hadn't taken your key or any money.'

He was *apologising* to her?

'I had a meeting which I couldn't not attend. Can you stand up?'

'I'm twenty-six, not eighty-six,' Gwynneth half joked. But nevertheless her semi-numbed legs, suffering the pins-and-needles burn of returning life, were glad of his help to support her as she struggled to stand up. He, of course, managed to uncoil himself from his hunkered-down position with enviable grace.

'Have you had anything to eat today?'

She shook her head. She wasn't sure she could cope with Tariq in this knight errant mood. It made her feel vulnerable, as though she was some kind of victim, and she didn't like that.

'So you haven't eaten since breakfast?' he demanded.

Gwynneth glared balefully at him as he unlocked the apartment door.

'Actually, no, I haven't. But there wasn't any need because I wasn't hungry. I had a big breakfast.'

'A yoghurt?'

'No one wants to eat much when it's hot.'

'No one?' His mouth twisted sardonically. That was more like it, she decided gratefully. 'By "no one", presumably you mean the British?' He was holding her arm, swinging her round to face him as he half dragged her into the hallway, pushing the door shut with one easy movement.

'You don't like us, do you?' she demanded. 'Why?'

'Congratulations on your powers of analysis,' Tariq told her sarcastically. 'As to why—that is my own business. But I certainly do not like the morals the young women of your country—of your type—adopt.'

Gwynneth glared at him. 'Do you know what?' she told him acerbically. 'You aren't just a bigot, you're a hypocrite as well.'

'Be careful,' Tariq warned her.

She was standing on that bridge again, Gwynneth knew. But she didn't seem able to stop herself.

'Of what? You? Why? In case you're tempted to do some close-up research into *my* morals? I wouldn't, if I were you.'

'Funny how sometimes a warning can sound more like an invitation,' Tariq derided her, adding unforgivably, 'You want me to take you to bed. We both know that.'

'We both know no such thing!' Gwynneth stormed back at him.

'It's the truth,' Tariq insisted, with another dismissive shrug of those powerful shoulders.

'I've never known any man as good at self-delusion as you!'

'And you've known a lot of men, of course,' he agreed smoothly.

Not in the Biblical sense, I haven't, Gwynneth was tempted to tell him. But a small inner voice warned her that that was a step too far right now. He might have already refused to believe she was still a virgin, but the mood he was in at the moment he might be tempted to *prove* to her that she wasn't. She knew he wouldn't force her, of course—the problem was that he wouldn't need to.

Hastily, she pointed out, 'Less than six hours ago I walked out of here rather than go to bed with you. Remember?'

'It was my decision not to proceed,' Tariq countered coolly. 'Whereupon you flounced out in a temper—no doubt expecting me to come after you and make you an offer you wouldn't want to refuse.'

The offer she wouldn't want to refuse from him would involve not money but a full bank account of sensual intimacy— a promise to pay in caresses and kisses that she could draw on whenever she felt the need.

Red-faced, Gwynneth shook herself free of her own dangerous thoughts.

'I have to go away for a few days,' Tariq told her abruptly. 'I shall be leaving later tonight. I have some business matters to attend to.' It was a four-hour drive at least to the valley, and he would normally have set out at dawn, but right now he ached for the solitude of the desert, with its infinite capacity to remind a man that his most basic struggle was that of survival. The desert was not a forgiving mistress; she made no allowances for human weakness in those who chose to embrace her. There, surely he would be able to see what he was experiencing for what it was—and that was a mere nothing. His desire for this woman whom he did not want to want was a minor inconvenience—a fire which would quickly burn itself out. He would call for police protection to ensure Chad's threats weren't carried out, and forget all about her.

Tariq had turned away from her, leaving Gwynneth free to watch him with hugely agonised dark eyes. He was going. He couldn't. He mustn't. She wanted him to stay here with her—she wanted him to stay with her for ever.

Gwynneth hadn't even realised she had made any sound at all until Tariq turned back to her, frowning as he demanded, 'What's wrong? You sound as though you are in pain.'

Her? In pain for him?

'That wasn't pain, it was relief,' she fibbed recklessly.

He gave her a taunting smile.

'I suggest that while I am away you give very serious thought to my offer to buy the apartment.' He looked at his watch again. 'It is now almost seven o'clock. I need to eat before I leave. I'm going to order in some food—for both of us.'

'I need to shower and change first,' Gwynneth protested.

'How long will that take you?'

'Twenty minutes—maybe half an hour.'

'Fine. I'll order the food for seven-thirty.'

He was walking away from her, leaving her standing there in the hallway, not even asking her if she had any preference as to what she wanted to eat. Gwynneth fumed. She had a good mind to tell him that she was perfectly capable of ordering her own food and that she preferred to eat alone rather than have her appetite ruined by his unwanted presence. That would be the only sensible thing to do, wouldn't it?

She was still refusing to answer that question ten minutes later as she stood under the shower, savouring the sensation of the water sluicing the detritus of the day from her skin. If only her heart could be as easily comforted and soothed.

* * *

The warmth of the water against his skin was almost as sensual as a woman's touch—which no doubt was why his thoughts were turning in a direction he did not wish them to go, and why his body was responding to those thoughts.

If he were holding her between his hands now, caressing her water-slick skin... Angrily Tariq turned the shower to 'cold', staying beneath it and willing it to douse the fire inside him. Had his father felt like this for his mother?

He reached up and switched off the shower. This was the first time he had allowed himself to think of his father in terms of his own experience. Like father, like son... But he had always sworn that he would never *allow* himself to be the son of the man who had given him life because of the way he had abandoned his mother. What had he been like? What would he see if he allowed his father to step out of the shadows into which he had thrust him?

He reached for a towel, his forehead furrowing as he tried to capture vague images of himself with his father as a child. Inside his head he could hear a faint echo of male laughter, feel the hard, sure warmth of paternal hands lifting him.

What had provoked this? It had to be her! How dared she look into his soul and disturb his secrets...?

He strode naked from the bathroom into his office, relieved to know that he wouldn't have to spend yet another night on the hugely uncomfortable sofabed. Quickly he pulled on clean clothes. No need to resume his headdress, since he was eating in the privacy of the apartment. He heard the door's security buzzer ring and checked his watch.

Twenty-five past seven.

If she wanted her food hot then she was going to have to hurry.

* * *

Was that the door she had just heard? Well, she was showered and dressed, in a black linen kaftan she had bought on impulse from a chainstore when she had seen it hanging on the reduced rail. She had plaited her damp hair for extra coolness, and put a slick of soft pink gloss on her lips. More important by far, she was very hungry. She opened her bedroom door and walked purposefully towards the kitchen.

The smell of the food was so deliciously appetising her stomach actually gave a small growl, causing her to place her hand against it and give Tariq a defiant look that melted in the heat of the sensual shock that hit her insides. He wasn't wearing his headdress, and his hair, like hers, was still damp, the sight of it unexpectedly erotic. Thick and cut short, more dark brown than black, it had a soft curl that made her long to slide her fingers into it and feel it curling round them. Beneath the hem of his robe she could see the indigo darkness of what looked like linen trousers of some description, whilst his feet were bare. For some reason that made her curl her own toes into her slip-on mules.

'I hope you like Lebanese food,' he told her. 'I ordered it for the variety. We can carry it out to the terrace; it will be pleasantly cool out there now.'

He certainly wasn't shy about giving orders, Gwynneth thought rebelliously, admitting at the same time that she was too hungry to waste time protesting. Instead she went to the cupboards, removing cutlery, plates and water glasses to put on a tray to carry outside, leaving Tariq to deal with the food.

The terrace was large enough to throw a party on, and seemed to have been equipped with just that in mind. Gwynneth put the tray down on a glass-topped low-level bamboo table and flicked on the light switch, which she discovered not only brought on the lights but activated an anti-mosquito unit as well.

Three long bamboo sofas, comfortably padded with cushions upholstered in a striking black, grey and off-white fabric, formed a U-shape around the table, so that one could look out over the balcony towards the sea.

Tariq had started to remove the lids from the food cartons, explaining as he did so, 'It is an Arab tradition for people to sit round what you would probably call a shared buffet, eating and talking, rather than to sit formally at a dining table.'

His gaze flicked over her as she stood by the balcony. The kaftan was obviously a deliberate ploy—but to what purpose?

'Come and eat while the food is still hot,' he commanded.

Without waiting to see if she would do so, he settled himself on one of the sofas, sitting cross-legged with enviable ease, the soles of his feet turned inward. Gwynneth remembered reading that it was considered a great insult to confront another man with the sole of one's foot or shoe.

It was impossible for her to match his fluid dexterity, so instead she sat primly opposite him with her feet placed firmly on the floor.

He paused in busily scooping up small amounts of food from the variety of containers to raise one eyebrow and drawl, 'Very proper, and I suspect most uncomfortable, but it's your choice.'

He had, Gwynneth noticed, used his fingers to remove the food, and was now dipping them into one of two bowls of water he must have brought out but which she hadn't previously noticed.

Hesitantly she inspected the contents of the containers, most of which she could recognise, and all of which smelled delicious.

'Spare ribs, chicken in herbs, couscous, taramasalata,' he

told her, naming several of the items as Gwynneth heaped her plate. She watched as Tariq used the flat unleavened pieces of bread to scoop up his food.

'I should have thought to ask if you wanted me to order you a bottle of wine. Since I'm going to be driving, alcohol is out for me.'

He saw her small questioning frown and added carelessly, as though it was of no great importance, 'I don't have any religious allegiance. My mother was Muslim but my father was British—and agnostic.'

'They must have loved one another very much to bridge that kind of cultural divide,' Gwynneth commented.

Tariq frowned. He had grown up hearing his father condemned, living with his mother's unhappiness, and now, abruptly, he realised that because of all that it had simply never occurred to him to think about how very much they must have once loved one another. How much…but still not enough.

But according to his second cousin it had been his mother whose love had weakened, not his father.

'Initially perhaps,'

'Initially?' Gwynneth queried.

'My parents separated when I was quite young,' he told her sombrely. 'Apparently they had an agreement that my father would live in my mother's country for the first few years and then she would move with him to his. She reneged on that agreement, so he left.'

'Oh, how dreadfully sad for all of you—but for you most especially,' Gwynneth sympathised.

Tariq shrugged dismissively. 'Not particularly. My mother moved back to live with her family, and I grew up surrounded by cousins and cousins of cousins. I lived very happily.'

'But you must have missed your father.'

'Why? Because you missed yours?'

'I missed both my parents,' Gwynneth told him, and then added honestly, 'Or rather, I missed sharing in what I imagined a happy family life would be. There is such a taboo surrounding the fact that mothers are not always able to love their children that people find it easier not to speak of it at all. I didn't myself for a long time.'

'So what changed?'

'I did. When I was able to accept that my mother hadn't loved me and equally able to accept that it wasn't my fault. I had to teach myself to accept that no one was to blame, and not just to accept that but to believe it as well.'

'And now you do?'

'Yes.'

'So will you have children yourself, or…?' Why was he talking to her like this? Asking her so many intimate and probing questions? Questions that went way beyond mere small talk. Why did he feel this deep, driving need to know everything there was to know about her, whether that knowledge related to her past experiences or her future plans? Too late, Tariq recognised just how much the questions he was asking her might reveal to her the feelings he had when he listened to her.

'It hasn't made me either hunger for them to rewrite my own childhood, nor fear the idea of them in case I repeat it with them, if that's what you mean. Were I to be in the right relationship with the right man…' She gave a small shrug, not daring to risk looking at him just in case he might see in her eyes the message her body was sending her. Right now, the only relationship it wanted her to have was with him! 'I do think women have a basic instinct and drive to have a child with the man they love; that way they can sub-consciously perhaps both possess a bit of him and leave a lasting memory of their love. But children are individuals and have to be respected as such. Perhaps that is where the danger can lie.'

Heavens, she was opening up to him more than she had ever done with anyone. Didn't her head know or care abut the danger her heart was facing? Tariq was watching her and lis-tening to her with a fixed concentration that made her heart hammer into her ribs as though it was trying to burst its way out of her chest and hurl itself into his arms.

'This is pretty deep stuff to discuss with a stranger,' she told him slightly breathlessly.

Stranger? She was right, of course; they were strangers to one another. And yet at some profoundly disturbing and deep level he felt so strongly connected to her... He pushed the thought away, barricading himself against it.

'Perhaps it is because we are strangers. Maybe it is with strangers that we feel most able to disclose our deepest thoughts and fears.' How could he be feeling like this about her when her values were so opposed to his own? She was a woman accustomed to the non-emotional, one-night stand type of sex; she was motivated by financial greed, as wit-nessed by the fact that she had refused his offer for the apart-ment, no doubt hoping to push the price up even further.

How could he even *think* about wanting her?

'Perhaps,' Gwynneth agreed. Whatever had existed between them over dinner to enable them to talk had now gone. She could sense it in the return of his coldness towards her.

'It's getting late, and I have a longish drive ahead of me—

so if you'll excuse me?' He spoke peremptorily, avoiding looking at her, standing up as easily and sinuously as he had sat down, whilst Gwynneth had to struggle somewhat to get up out of her cushioned comfort.

Had she bored and irritated him by spilling out her most personal thoughts to him like that? She tensed as he came towards her, leaning down to help her to her feet. In the small enclosed space between the sofa and the table they had to stand virtually body-to-body. He smelled of something cool and pleasant, but her senses were reacting to the more dangerous male scent of him that lay under it. Instinctively she closed her eyes, the better to focus on it, swaying slightly towards him.

Tariq exhaled fiercely. He could see the stiffness of her nipples silhouetted against the fabric of her kaftan and he had to clench his free hand into a fist to stop himself from lifting it to touch her. Her plaited hair exposed the vulnerability of the nape of her neck, tempting him to trace the shape of her bones with his lips and follow them down the length of her back, whilst his hands plundered the female curves of her breast and belly before...

The minute she felt the heat of Tariq's breath on her neck Gwynneth snapped her eyes open and stepped back from him, her face on fire with guilt.

How long would he be gone? For her own sake she hoped it would be long enough for the Zurani officials to untangle the complex ownership issues relating to the apartment. She desperately wanted to draw a line under the entire proceedings.

But not so desperately that she was willing to accept Tariq's offer?

That was because she didn't feel she could trust him—because her gut instinct told her that he had some kind of other agenda she wasn't aware of. Did it matter if he had? she asked herself as he released her arm and bent to start collecting the empty food cartons, stacking them on the tray.

Yes, it *did* matter, if that agenda involved money. Not for herself, but for Teresa and Anthony.

CHAPTER TEN

GWYNNETH shook her hair back off her face as she stepped out of the lift and headed for the apartment. She had been awake so early that she had decided to go for an early-morning run while it was still cool enough to do so. But although the exercise might have strengthened her body, it certainly hadn't strengthened her defences against her feelings for Tariq.

Tariq. She was getting dangerously close to living, breathing, thinking Tariq one hundred per cent of her time, and it didn't take a mathematical wizard to work out that that added up to loving him one hundred per cent.

Panic started to grip her. She must not love him. Not when he so patently did not love her. But he wanted her; it filled the space between them, infusing it with a predatory male sexual urgency that left her breathless, her heart pounding, as though the air had been robbed of oxygen.

This was crazy. She reached for her mobile in order to ring the young land registry official to find out what was happening, sighing when, instead of a human voice, she got his mechanised answering service, requesting her to leave a message. Leave a message? Saying what, exactly? That she had been offered twice the value of the apartment to relinquish her claim on it, but she was concerned about the validity of the offer and even more concerned that the apartment wouldn't be the only thing Tariq might steal from her.

Tariq. Where was he? What was he doing? What was he thinking? Was he thinking about her at all? Had he missed her last night? She had certainly missed him. Her hand trembled as she filled the kettle.

Her thoughts still on Tariq, Gwynneth browsed the bookshelves in his office, looking for something to read. She hesitated, torn between the book she had already read on Zuran and its history and what looked like a rather heavy book on the geological formation of the desert. Perhaps it wouldn't be as dull as it looked. As she removed it from the shelf she realised that another much thinner paperback book had been wedged behind it. Automatically she picked it up, intending to replace it, stopping when she saw the title: *Mjenat: The Hidden Valley and its Ruler.*

A book about the Hidden Valley? Smiling happily, she abandoned her original choice and headed for the terrace with her find.

Less than five minutes later the smile had disappeared from her face and she was sitting bolt upright, a look of angry disbelief widening her eyes as she stared at the photograph inside the front cover of the book.

Tariq! Or, to give him correct title, she corrected herself bitterly, His Highness Prince Tariq bin Salud Al Fwaisa. Tariq wasn't just Tariq, but a prince. And not just any old prince, either: he was the ruler of his own small kingdom.

On the opposite page to the photograph was a glowing tribute to him, and a discreet mention of his billionaire status not quite hidden in the flowery language giving thanks for his generosity to others.

Gwynneth threw the book down and went to the edge of the terrace, blinking back angry tears as she stared over the balcony.

Why hadn't he said something—anything? Why had he let her think…?

Did she *really* need to ask herself that question? she derided herself scornfully. He hadn't told her because men like him did not tell women like her—women they slept with once and then discarded, women they thought of as merely objects—*anything*. They didn't have a need to do so, and they certainly didn't have the desire to do so. Such men were users, and to them women like her were merely there to be exploited and then forgotten—women to be bought, played with for a while and then thrown out with the rubbish.

Only Tariq had not been able to do that with her, because she had refused to be thrown out of the apartment. He, no doubt wary of attracting unwanted attention to his off-duty pursuits, had had to resort to other measures by which to be rid of her. Measures such as offering her twice the value of the apartment. In order to get rid of her. That was all he wanted— to get rid of her! The pain caught her off guard, smashing through her anger and driving a stake right through her heart.

'And we think we've located the source of the underground spring that fills the oasis,' one of the team of scientists Tariq was employing on his Hidden Valley project told him excitedly. 'It looks as though it's fed by an overspill from something else—either a lake or maybe even a river. We already know that there's some kind of a cave formation beneath that outcrop of rocks at the head of the valley, below the foundations of the original palace.'

'It would have made sense to build a fortification around such a spring, to ensure that water would still be available in a siege situation—especially since at the time the original palace was built the valley lay close to one of the main camel train routes. Taking possession of the valley and its oasis meant my ancestors would have had both a financial asset and a need to protect it.' As he spoke, Tariq couldn't help thinking about Gwynneth, and the way she had reacted to his offer to buy the apartment from her.

'It strikes me,' Hal Derwent, chief archaeologist for the group, put in, 'that we could be looking at a situation where, if there are underground caves and passages, these could have been utilised to provide an escape route from the fortress if necessary—maybe even via the environs of the oasis in some way. This land, the desert, has always fascinated me. It holds so many secrets and gives them up so reluctantly.'

'Perhaps that is why my people think of the desert as female,' Tariq told him dryly.

'The earth's inner space is equally as fascinating as outer space—more so as far as I'm concerned,' Hal remarked, adding ruefully, 'What I could do with a tithe of a space exploration budget!'

'Well, I can't promise you that,' Tariq told him. 'But it may be that with the help of neighbouring countries we could investigate further. However, as you know, preserving the environment of the area's flora and fauna is of prime importance to me.'

'And me,' chimed in Bob Holmes, the team's natural history professor. 'Because the oasis is on private land which is virtually cut off from the rest of the desert, and not on any of the old camel trading routes, from a natural history point of view it is totally unique. I'm particularly interested in some of the species of fish we've taken from the oasis. They look like the kind of tropical saltwater fish you would expect to find on a coral reef, but the oasis is *not* salt water—even though its rock formation does provide a form of reef environment for them.'

Tariq smiled. 'There is a story that a long-ago prince built a private courtyard garden for his favourite houri, complete with a large glass tank filled with small reef fish. When the concubine died, after being poisoned by a rival, the Prince had the tank removed because he was unable to bear the sight of something that reminded him so painfully of the woman he had loved and lost. He gave orders that the tank and the fish were to be destroyed, but the young daughter of one of the men doing the work loved the fish so much she persuaded her father to help her remove them from the tank and place them in the oasis, praying to Allah as she did so that they might live.' He gave a small shrug. 'Who knows? Just as the flesh of a peach holds the kernel that is its seed, maybe there is an element of truth in the story, and the fish in the oasis are the offspring of saltwater fish who managed to survive and adapt.'

'Possibly. Or perhaps some seabird, or even a trained falcon, caught fish out over the gulf and then accidentally dropped its prey here.'

Tariq raised one eyebrow.

'Yes, it does sound pretty far-fetched.' Bob laughed. 'But one never knows.'

With summer setting in and the temperature rising steeply, all work on the valley had ceased. Tariq had not wanted to risk disturbing its animal life by setting up arc lighting so that the men could work in the cool hours of the night. The contractors were now securing the sites, ready to leave later in the day. He still had to talk to the men working on the excavation of the site of the original palace, and on the restoration of its hanging gardens, but instead of his thoughts being totally focused on this project which meant so much to him he was finding that they kept escaping from his control, subtly drifting away so that they could embrace Gwynneth Talbot. As he himself also ached to do?

With a brief nod to the other men he strode towards the villa where he and his parents had lived until their separation, unlocking the door and tensing as he stopped inside into the welcome dark coolness.

The villa had been built by his grandfather following the time-honoured principles of Middle Eastern architecture—which were to ensure that as much cool air as possible was drawn into a home and as much hot sunshine as possible kept out.

The villa was a solidly structured four-square building, enclosing four inner courtyards, three of which were gardens. Each corner of the building possessed a traditional wind tower, looking out across the desert and inward to the gardens beyond. An image slid into his head—a mental picture of himself with his father. He would have been about three, or maybe even four, clinging tightly to his father's hand as they climbed the stairs to one of the wind towers. His father, he remembered now, had looked out across the desert as he explained to him the principles behind their construction. Longing for his freedom? Or simply yearning for a broader horizon he could share with his wife and son?

His mother had said nothing to him of the promise his second cousin had described. But she, unlike his father, had craved the inner seclusion of the garden courtyards. Even when they had gone to live in Zuran she had preferred the solitude of her own company. Because—as he had always believed—of her grief at his father's betrayal? Or because, quite simply, she'd been a solitary person who had preferred to stand apart from others, as he did himself sometimes?

It was here that his father had taught him to play football and to read English, and here too that the older man had stood and watched quietly whilst Tariq had received his first lessons in the art of falconry. So many memories he hadn't previously allowed himself to acknowledge. Doing so now in the light of what he had learned was hauntingly bittersweet.

The apartment was silent and empty. It was gone midnight, but Gwynneth felt too restless and on edge to go to bed. Instead she went out onto the terrace. Was it really only yesterday that she and Tariq had eaten here together? Or rather, she and His Highness Prince Tariq bin Salud Al Fwaisa, she corrected herself grimly. No wonder she had thought him arrogant.

Someone on another balcony had been burning incense, and its heavy sensual scent was conjuring up images of a wide low-lying divan and night air softly wafting shadowy, gauzy fabrics. The East was all about the senses, Gwynneth decided; it reached out to all of them in ways that one didn't experience in the West.

There was a small shop in the souk where one could buy a wide range of different scents and the burners, and she was tempted to make a purchase there herself. For what purpose? So that when she went home she could light the burner and remember this and Tariq? She wasn't going to need any sensory aids to prompt her memory.

Tariq, who was no doubt ready to pay her anything so that he could get her out of his life!

Was that why he was so determined to keep this apartment? Because he came here to have sex with women, and needed it for the anonymity it afforded him? It all added up—right down to the way he had behaved towards her that first night.

Tariq—she refused to mentally address him any other way, she decided belligerently—used this apartment to have sex with women chosen either by himself or, even more unpalatably, on his behalf. Its anonymity here in the heart of Zuran's hotel quarter meant it was ideally suited for his needs. Although no doubt he could afford to buy others, plainly he did not wish to waste time or energy doing so. It was easier simply to buy her out, even if that meant he had to pay over the market price. What was an extra £500,000 to a man she now knew to be one of Zuran's wealthier billionaires?

Gwynneth paced the terrace, her face burning and her thoughts in turmoil. It made her skin crawl with loathing to know what the apartment really was, and to know too that she was simply another piece of female flesh who had been processed through it for a cold-hearted too-rich man's pleasure. She had been idiotically naïve, thinking that just because she felt shocked at wanting a man she barely knew, was tormented by the intensity of that wanting, Tariq must in some way be experiencing the male equivalent of her feelings. That he, like her, must be questioning the inappropriateness of their mutual desire at the same time as he was compelled to acknowledge the sheer force of it. That was the trouble with being an ageing virgin who didn't have the physical or emotional experience to recognise the reality of how modern sexual mores translated into real life.

She deplored her foolish belief that they shared a mutual but inadmissible and unspoken itch for one another they had been equally driven to scratch and equally infuriated by. They were not and never had been equals of any kind. In Tariq's eyes she was simply a piece of human flesh he'd wanted to use, he had used, and no doubt he would use many more pieces.

She derided herself for actually thinking that Tariq's reaction had been the male emotional stereotype. There had no emotional input into his reaction to her at all other than that of arrogant disbelief and anger.

And she had left it too late to defend herself from the fallout—the humiliation of recognising that whilst she had engaged with him emotionally, physically and mentally, he had simply thought of her in terms of his own sexual satisfaction. The truth was that he had put about as much emotional effort into her as he would have done eating a fast-food meal—probably less.

That was what you got from sexually locking yourself away from modern life. Another woman of her age, wiser to the reality of things than she was, would no doubt have known immediately what his agenda was.

Of course he wanted to get rid of her. She was cramping his style.

And he was breaking her heart.

She stiffened, recoiling from her thoughts, but they wouldn't be denied. Tariq breaking her heart? That just wasn't possible. He had made her feel desire, yes. But desire was only physical. What she *felt* for him was only physical. It had to be.

She had to get away from him, and she had to put this whole episode totally behind her.

When he came back she would tell him that she had

changed her mind and that she was willing to accept his offer.
Then she would move out of the apartment and into the most
inexpensive hotel she could find—if there was such a thing
as an inexpensive hotel in Zuran—and she would stay there
until the formalities had been completed and Tariq's money
was safely in the bank account she had already opened to hold
the money from her father's estate.

Tariq frowned as he studied his computer screen. He was supposed to be dealing with a backlog of correspondence and
updating his files with regard to the fact that work in the
valley had now ceased until the cooler weather. Instead of
which he was wasting time thinking about Gwynneth and
wondering how much thought his parents had given to the
problems their different outlooks on life, and the manner in
which they'd wanted to live it, could cause them before they
had decided to get married. Or hadn't they given any thought
to those problems at all? Had they simply assumed that their
love was strong enough to overcome them?

If he left here now he could be back in Zuran before dawn.
But to what purpose? To wake Gwynneth from her sleep with
the touch of his hands and his mouth? To take from her her
words of denial and change them into soft sounds of delight?

He was crazy for thinking like this. The discovery that his
father had not been the contemptible figure he had always believed was not a licence for him to start believing that…

That what? That he did not need to fight against what he
was feeling anymore? What he was *feeling*—was he crazy?
She had made it plain by her behaviour that she relished the
danger of sex with strangers, and with ever-changing partners.
The woman he committed to would have to be his exclu-

sively and for ever, no matter what her past sexual lifestyle had been. There would have to be honesty and openness between them, a desire to understand and to bridge any cultural and emotional differences. Perhaps most importantly of all, the woman sharing his life would have to understand and support the fact that he had a duty to his heritage—to its past, its present and its future.

He looked towards the narrow window which gave on to the main courtyard where his 4x4 was parked. He could be back at the apartment in four hours. Less if he pushed himself.

He got up and went to stand by the window, looking down into the courtyard. And what if he did go back and make love to her? What then? All he would be doing was taking another step towards an end that was inevitable—because ultimately any relationship they had *would* end. The leopard couldn't change its spots, nor the falcon cease to fly. He knew himself well enough to know that he would not be able to live with the fear that ultimately she would leave him. Better the sharp agony of self-denial now than the long, slow putrefying death of his self-respect and pride.

He turned away from the window and went back to the computer.

CHAPTER ELEVEN

IT MIGHT be early, but she was far from the only person up and about, Gwynneth realised as she paid for the carton of milk she had hurried out to buy. No way could she drink black coffee, and no way could she face Tariq's return without the mind-sharpening protection of her regular caffeine fix.

As she made her way back to the apartment she was vaguely aware of a car crawling along the side of the quiet side street virtually beside her, but she was too busy worrying about how she was going to cope with seeing Tariq to do more than glance idly at it.

She had almost reached the apartment block when, suddenly and terrifyingly, the two men who had been casually walking behind her abruptly closed the distance, trapping her between them, grabbing hold of her and dragging her over to the now stationary car. Zuran was famed for the safety of its holidaymakers, and Gwynneth hadn't given a thought to the danger of walking around on her own because it hadn't occurred to her that there was any.

She struggled frantically to break free of her captors as she saw the rear passenger door of the car being thrust open.

They were on the point of pushing her into the car, virtually head first, when out of nowhere—or so it seemed to Gwynneth—three police cars screeched up, blocking in her would-be kidnappers. Their doors were flung open to allow half a dozen or more armed policemen to come running to her aid, so that within seconds of being grabbed she was free and her assailants were being marched to the waiting police cars in handcuffs, along with the driver of the car.

'It is fortunate that we happened to be driving past and saw what was happening,' the most senior-looking of the policemen told Gwynneth, after he had assured himself that she was all right, if very shocked, and she had thanked him for their timely appearance. 'Where were you going?' he asked.

Gwynneth inclined her head in the direction of the apartment building.

'One of my men will escort you back to your apartment,' he informed her.

A brief nod of his head brought not one but two thick-set police officers to her side. To her bemusement, they not only escorted her all the way back to the apartment, they also insisted on coming inside with her and on checking every single room.

Who needed caffeine? Gwynneth thought shakily once they had gone and reaction had begun to set in. She was having to fight against a very strong desire to sit down and have a good cry. Shock, she told herself pragmatically. It was just the effects of delayed shock. Perhaps she should have that coffee after all.

Tariq had left the valley just before dawn, watching the sun bring colour and light to the desert, turning the sand from grey to an almost blinding silver gilt.

The mobile he used for business was switched off, but the phone for his private line to the Ruler was as always on. He was an hour out of Zuran when it shrilled sharply, and he frowned and pulled up to take the call.

The Chief of Police was brief and matter-of-fact. Thanks to the round-the-clock surveillance he had put in place at the apartment, his men had already circumvented two attacks on Ms Gwynneth Talbot.

'What kind of attacks?' Tariq demanded.

'The first was an attempt to run her down in the street. They may only have intended to scare her; who can say? The second, though, was definitely more serious. They were attempting to kidnap her. We are currently questioning the men involved, who have admitted working for Rheinvelt. We think we have all the plotters now, but to be on the safe side, Highness, I would respectfully request that Ms Talbot move into a safe house until we are sure.'

He only had a heartbeat in which to make his decision, but that was all he needed. It was as simple as that—and as easy. Between one heartbeat and the next he had made up his mind.

'That won't be necessary,' he said crisply. 'I am on my way back to the apartment now, and when I leave later today to return to Mjenat Ms Talbot will be accompanying me. She will be safe there.'

'I shall have my men post a guard on the road to the Valley, Highness. Although I admit that I cannot think of anywhere safer for her. If these men we are questioning now are telling the truth, then we have all those involved in custody now, and the fact that they have been apprehended and will be punished according to Zurani law should stand as a warning to anyone else your friend might try to hire in their place. Our Esteemed

Ruler has made it plain that he will not tolerate Zuran being corrupted by money-laundering or other illicit activities, and that a clear message must be sent out to anyone who doubts his determination on the matter, so he will not be inclined to deal lightly with them.'

After he had ended the call and restarted the 4x4, Tariq discovered that his hands were shaking. His heart thudded impatiently into his chest wall, urging him to get to Gwynneth as fast as he possibly could. He should never have left her on her own, exposed to such danger. Any thoughts he might have had of sending her back to her home country had gone. There was only one place he wanted her to be from now on, and that was with him. He was finally prepared to admit that to himself.

Gwynneth had packed her case, and was ready to leave just as soon as she had informed Tariq that she was now prepared to accept his offer. When would he be back?

This would be the last time she would see him. Good. That was what she wanted.

Liar, liar! she mocked herself.

All right then, she mentally amended, to appease that inner knowing voice, it was what she needed! Satisfied? she asked her inner critic.

It was Friday, and Zuran City was busy with worshippers coming from the city's mosques as Tariq nosed the big vehicle down the same side street where earlier Gwynneth had so nearly been abducted. He drove down into the underground car park, leaving the 4x4 parked next to the new baby Bentley he preferred if he was driving himself in town. Unlike the other male members of his extended family, Tariq lived his life free of any kind of personal retinue as much as he could.

The service lift took him up to the apartment, where he slid his key card into the lock and thrust open the door.

Gwynneth was pacing the terrace, mentally rehearsing the speech she had tailored to be as brief as she could make it. She hadn't heard Tariq arrive and so he had the leisure to watch her for several seconds without her knowing that he was doing so.

It was some sixth sense that alerted her to his presence— a sharp surge of awareness that drew her gaze into the shadows where he stood as speedily as a she-falcon returning to the lure.

Tariq strode over to the terrace and stepped onto it to join her.

'There is something I want to say to you.'

'Really? Like what? A repeat of that offer you made me for this apartment? One million pounds? Why not make it two—after all, you can afford can't you, Your Highness? And before you try to deny it, I've read all about you in *this*!' she informed him, throwing the book onto the seating.

She had promised herself she wouldn't do this—so why, oh, why was she doing it? Dignified silence, that was how she had intended to greet him—and leave him. And now look at her, ranting and raving like a jealous lover!

That book! He had forgotten it even existed, and he cursed even more now than he had done when he had first discovered it had been written. But his pain was greater than his anger.

'Two million? Why stop at that?' he demanded bitingly. He could overlook much, but not this kind of greed. Not and still call himself a man. His heart felt as though it was being wrenched apart. 'Why not ask for three million? Or four? But let me tell you, if you do, the answer will be the same—and it is no. Contrary to what you seem to think, the fact that I am who I am does not make me a soft touch for greedy amoral women. I've already offered you more than this place is worth.'

'Yes, I know that.' Gwynneth stopped him. 'And I know why.'

Tariq watched her. Had one of the men the Chief of Police had sent to guard her broken with security protocol and told her why she was being guarded?

'No wonder you want to pay me to guarantee your own exclusive secret ownership of this place. Having me here must have been cramping your style!' Gwynneth burst out. 'It wasn't very hard for me to work it all out once I knew who you are. You use this apartment as…as your own private brothel—that's why you mistook me for a prostitute! And you had the gall to question *my* morals!'

She mustn't let him see how upset she was.

'Not that any of that matters now,' she added, getting her voice under control. How could she lie to herself like this? It mattered more than anything else in the whole of her life, just as *he* mattered more than anything or anyone else. 'I've decided to accept your offer and to sell you the apartment, but… but only at the real market price.'

She had really had to battle with herself over that. There was no way she would want to be paid more if she only had herself to consider, but by accepting less than he was prepared to pay she was depriving Teresa and Anthony of a considerable sum of money. But morally she could not bring herself to accept more than the apartment was worth—not even for them. And besides, £500,000 was still a very respectable nest egg.

'So perhaps we can just get on with things and get all the paperwork sorted out as quickly as possible,' she continued briskly. 'I'm prepared to move out of here until everything's done.'

Tariq shrugged dismissively, as though her words—like her feelings, no doubt—meant nothing to him.

'I'm afraid that isn't going to be possible now,' he told her.

Gwynneth stared at him, and then stammered, 'What—what do you mean?' Had he changed his mind and decided to buy somewhere else?

Tariq gestured towards the cane sofas, saying authoritatively, 'We may as well sit down.'

Reluctantly Gwynneth perched on the corner of the nearest seat, tensing when Tariq came and sat next to her, his long legs splayed out in front of him, his thigh touching her own. She wanted desperately to move away from him, but she was trapped against the side of the sofa with nowhere to go.

'First, allow me to correct your misapprehensions. Contrary to what you seem to imagine, my way of life does not include semi-clandestine sexual liaisons. Nor do I have any desire for it to do so.'

'You expect me to believe that, after—?'

'After what?' Tariq pressed her smoothly. 'After I allowed you to tempt me?'

'I did not tempt you! You were the one who—' Gwynneth took a deep breath and shook her head. 'Look, all I want—all I came here for—is to sell the apartment and take the money home with me.'

'Money is obviously very important to you,' he agreed unkindly.

Anger flashed in Gwynneth's eyes.

'Actually, you're wrong. It isn't. But on this occasion—'

'On this occasion you thought you would allow it to matter?'

'No! If I only had myself to consider I'd walk out of here right now and let you keep the wretched thing.'

'If you only had yourself to consider? And what exactly does that mean?' Tariq queried.

Gwynneth closed her eyes and then opened them again. 'If you must know…'

'I must,' Tariq confirmed grimly.

Gwynneth took a deep breath and began quietly, 'My father had a…a girlfriend. Teresa. And a baby—Anthony. My half-brother.' She could sense that Tariq was looking at her, but she refused to return his look, determinedly focusing her gaze away from him as she continued. 'Prior to his death, Dad came to England on business and he brought Teresa and their baby back with him. He introduced them to me. Until then I hadn't even realised they existed, but that was Dad all over. There'd been so many women in and out of his life for so long that I never thought…' She gave a small shrug, not wanting to stray into the painful history of her relationship with her father. 'Originally Teresa was from the Philippines. From what she's told me, it's obvious that her family have very little in the way of material assets. She wants to go back there and bring Anthony up. Even a little money would make a huge difference to their lives, but since my father hadn't changed his will, and they weren't married, he hadn't made any provision for her. Everything was left to me. The apartment was his only major asset, and I decided to sell it and to put the money in trust for Teresa and Anthony. That's why I came here.'

She heard Tariq's sharp intake of breath but she still refused to look at him.

'You want the money for someone else?' he demanded.

'Yes,' Gwynneth confirmed simply. Pride strengthened her voice as she told him, 'I don't need or want my father's money. I've supported myself financially since I left university, and to be quite frank I prefer it that way. All I ever wanted from my father was his love.' What on earth had made her tell him that?

'It seems to me that you and I share an emotional burden,' he said quietly. 'Problems with our fathers left over from the pain of our childhoods.'

Now she did look at him, unable to stop herself from doing so. What she could see in his eyes made her heart tighten with pain—his pain this time, though, not her own. She didn't speak. Not wanting to in case she broke the fragile bond Tariq was so unexpectedly creating between them with his confidences.

'I had always believed—been told—that my father abandoned my mother when I was quite young,' he told her. 'I only recently learned about the extenuating circumstances of which I spoke to you. After so many years of seeing my father as a man to despise and dislike, wanting to deny my cultural heritage from him, it is an odd sensation to realise that I may not have known the truth—that I misjudged him.'

Gwynneth swallowed against her own bittersweet emotions. Bitter because of her memories, and sweet because Tariq was confiding in her. 'I wish I could say the same about my own father,' she admitted. 'Unfortunately I have always known the reality of what he was, because he always made a point of telling me.'

Tariq could hear the stark sadness in her voice.

'But you are still prepared to put your life on hold in order to help his girlfriend and child?'

'They are not my father. And besides, despite everything, somehow I feel I owe it to him as well as them to do everything that I can for them.' She gave a small sigh. 'He wasn't a bad man so much as a selfish, amoral one.'

'Amoral?'

'He was very highly sexed,' Gwynneth told him bluntly. 'And he liked to talk about his conquests and his prowess.' She saw the way Tariq was frowning, and, realising too late the interpretation he must be putting on her admission, corrected it hastily, assuring him, 'Oh, not in any kind of abusive way.'

'For an adult to impose his sexuality on a child in any kind of way, even verbally, is abusive,' Tariq said grimly.

With a father who had boasted to her about his sexuality, perhaps it was no wonder that she herself was sexually promiscuous, he reflected. Maybe she had even felt subconsciously that she had to compete with her father in order to win his approval.

'That is why the apartment is so important to me,' Gwynneth repeated, unaware of the way in which he had interpreted her words. 'Because of Teresa and Anthony.'

'You have been honest and open with me. Now it is my turn to be equally open and honest with you,' Tariq informed her gravely. 'Prior to your arrival here in Zuran I was involved in an undercover operation to discover the identity of the leader of a criminal gang who were targeting Zuran with a variety of criminal activities—including the double-selling scam, which enabled them to launder money. In that role I had to pretend that I was prepared to assist the gang with the necessary legalities in exchange for a financial interest in the racket. As a sweetener they gave me this apartment, so in the interests of realism I had to be seen to be using it. The night I found you here I had been offered the reward of a night with one of the prostitutes they hoped to establish here in Zuran. I had turned that offer down, but when I found you here, I thought….'

'That I was a prostitute,' Gwynneth supplied for him. 'It's okay. You don't need to apologise,' she added flippantly, in an attempt to conceal the surge of giddily relieved joy foaming up inside her. 'I'll take it as read.'

'As to that, I wasn't aware that I had anything to apologise for,' Tariq informed her coolly. 'I may have been in error with regard to your professional status, but you made it very clear that you were enjoying what was happening.'

She couldn't argue with that, Gwynneth realised, but she still struggled to defend herself, protesting, 'That was a mistake! I wasn't… I didn't…'

She could see from the way he was looking at her that she wasn't having the effect she wanted to have. She might as well give up, she acknowledged, because she certainly wasn't going to tell him that her reaction to him had trashed every single conviction she had had about her own sexuality.

Instead she gave him a bright, determined smile and said lightly, 'Well, now that we've cleared the air, and we both know what the real situation is, I'll find a hotel to book into. I'm already packed—'

'No.'

'No?' Ridiculously, her heart was beating far too fast, and with far, far too much pleasure—as though it had interpreted his refusal as a sign that he wanted her to stay with him. How on earth had that happened? She had thought she had endured enough to be protected from the danger of that kind of emotional responsiveness to him.

'We're leaving for Mjenat immediately. The Hidden Valley,' he explained. 'We shall be staying there for the foreseeable future.'

He was taking her to his home. He wanted her with him. He wanted her. A second rush of joyful exhilaration followed the first before she could control it, telling its own story—as if she needed to be told how she felt about him.

'But…'

'I'm afraid there is no alternative. You are in too much danger to remain here in Zuran.'

She blinked at him. 'Danger?'

'Yes. I regret to say that because you have been seen entering and leaving this apartment you have become vulnerable. The Zurani Chief of Police has received information that hitmen have been hired to…punish me for my part in ensuring that the gang are not able to set up their operations in Zuran. He has warned me that anyone closely connected with me is at risk. In fact he rang me this morning to tell me that his men have already foiled two attempts to harm you.'

Gwynneth suddenly felt quite sick with shock and disbelief.

'The car…and then those men…' she whispered.

'Yes,' Tariq agreed. 'Fortunately the Chief of Police has his men keeping a watchful eye on you. These people obviously think that you are my lover, and that is why they are targeting you. The Chief of Police believes that they now have all those involved under lock and key, but he has said that he wants some more time to be totally sure. It is for that reason that you and I are going to the Valley. You will be safe there.'

Safe? With him? What a fool she had been to have thought…what she had thought. And how revealing her reaction had been. How had it happened that she had allowed herself to become so emotionally vulnerable to him? All her life she had guarded herself against just that kind of danger, yet now, and with a man her common sense should have told her was not for her, she had somehow or other let him into her heart. And now it was too late to try to bar it to him. Much too late. And *that* meant…

The enormity of what it meant made her feel sick and shaky. She couldn't go anywhere with him. Not now that she could no longer hide from the fact that she had fallen in love with him. And especially not now when she knew that he did not return that love. 'There's no need for me to go anywhere with you,' she told him unsteadily. 'I can go home. I'll be safe there.'

'Maybe. Maybe not. And I am not prepared to take the risk of that "maybe not".'

'You are not prepared?' She was using her anger to drive away those other feelings she must not feel. 'I am an adult, and I am perfectly capable of making up my own mind and taking my own decisions.'

'Indeed. But you must understand that I have a moral duty to protect you, since it is because of me that you are in danger. Were I to allow you to leave Zuran, I would have to send men with you to guard you.'

He obviously wasn't joking about the potential danger, Gwynneth saw apprehensively.

'But your Chief of Police said he's got those responsible,' she pointed out doggedly.

'I said he believes that he has. Naturally he wants to be totally sure.'

'But surely it isn't really necessary for me to go to the Valley with you?'

'Unfortunately, I'm afraid that it is.'

So in actual fact he *didn't* want her with him. She assimilated that information in silence as she fought down the pain it brought her. The truth was that she wanted to go with him as little as he wanted her to be there—although for a very different reason. She had felt much safer when the barrier between them had been her assumption about his way of life and her aversion to it. Then she had believed that, no matter how physically tempted by him she might be, her emotional revulsion to what he represented would keep her safe.

Now she was having to accept that he was a man of principle and integrity. And the only barrier she had to protect her was his lack of any real emotional interest in her.

But that was all the barrier she needed, wasn't it? After all, she wasn't going to throw herself at him! What would she say? *Take me—oh, and by the way, I'm still a virgin, even if you've refused to believe me, and now I get to prove it to you.*

'I appreciate your concern,' she told him, trying to sound as cool and professional as she could. 'But I'm sure I will be perfectly safe once I get home.'

'I can't afford to take the chance that you won't be,' Tariq informed her bluntly. 'You may be aware that Zuran is investing its oil revenues in developing the country as a resort and sports destination. In order for us to succeed we need to be able to assure visitors of their safety. If you were to be followed home and attacked in some way it wouldn't be very long before it became linked to your visit here. That could have an adverse effect on our reputation.'

She couldn't argue against what he was saying, Gwynneth knew, and, although she hated admitting it, what he had told her had left her feeling vulnerable and uneasy. He was plainly not going to give in—which meant that she would have to.

'How long would I have to stay with you?' she asked him with resignation.

'Not long. A matter of a few days—a week at the most. The Chief of Police is virtually sure that they have all those involved in custody now. He simply wants to double check.'

Gwynneth lifted her shoulders in a small shrug of defeat. 'Very well. Mjenat has a fascinating history. In different circumstances I would have enjoyed visiting it, especially in view of your project to recreate the hanging gardens.'

'Work in the valley has finished now, until the cooler weather returns. I do not want to disturb the wildlife by lighting the area at night, but I confess I am impatient to move things forward. It was my father's idea originally, and I am sorry that he will never see the end result.'

'It will be a wonderful testimony to him, though, won't it?' Gwynneth said quietly. 'To both your parents, in fact. To create something so beautiful and fragile in such a hostile environment calls for a tremendous act of faith.'

'The same could well be said of love within marriage,' Tariq told her softly.

Gwynneth looked at him. He was looking back at her. Suddenly she felt as though a subtle emotional change of gear had taken place. The silence they had been filling with their conversation had somehow deepened and almost wrapped itself around them, locking them together in a dangerous intimacy. If he came to her now…

But he didn't. Instead he stood up and said dismissively, as though he couldn't even feel it, 'We need to leave as soon as we can.'

CHAPTER TWELVE

'I'M AFRAID we're going to have to fend for ourselves whilst we're here. My housekeeper and her husband are away on holiday,' Tariq informed Gwynneth,

They were in Mjenat, standing in the main courtyard to a large villa, having arrived only a few minutes earlier.

'I'll just deactivate the alarm system and then we can go in.'

Gwynneth studied her surroundings covertly. A high perimeter wall protected both the villa's privacy and its security. She had seen the discreetly placed security cameras as they drove into the valley itself, and Tariq had informed her that the collection of buildings just inside the valley were normally used to house those working there but that half a dozen policemen were already in residence there, along with back-up personnel to make sure that they didn't get any unwanted visitors.

His words were a reminder to her of just who and what he was.

'I suppose that by rights I ought to be addressing you by your title,' she commented, as he pushed open the high arched wooden doors.

'I don't use it—other than on State occasions or when my second cousin insists,' he told her matter-of-factly, adding,

'I don't see the need. A man should surely be able to command the respect of others by virtue of his own acts, or not at all.'

The interior of the villa, cool and shadowy after the heat outside, smelled faintly of incense and roses.

'I will take you to the women's quarters. Please follow me.'

The women's quarters. The words conjured up images of sloe-eyed concubines waiting dutifully to please their master.

'The villa was built for my grandfather, and after my father's death my mother chose to live as a traditional Muslim woman, keeping to her own quarters.'

'But what about you? Were you allowed to live there with her?'

He stopped walking to turn round and look at her, frowning slightly. Her question, with its obviously genuine concern, had caught him off guard. Listening to it, hearing the almost maternal anxiety of a woman for a child, touched gently on the painful bruises of his childhood which now as a man he preferred to forget he had once felt. And yet there was something sweetly healing and tender about hearing the emotion in Gwynneth's voice legitimise his childhood pain.

'I went to live in the palace in Zuran, where I became part of a household in which there were many other children,' he answered her lightly. 'As was the custom then, we were cared for by others.'

In other words he had been abandoned by his parents in much the same way as she had been abandoned by hers. Without thinking, she reached out to touch his arm in an automatic gentle gesture of compassion. To her shock just the simple act of her fingertips brushing against his robe-covered forearm made her heart lurch against her ribs and her belly turn to liquid female heat. Her reasons for touching him were forgotten as she was overwhelmed by a need to slide her hand beneath the fabric of his sleeve so that she could stroke her fingertips through the soft furring of hair on his arm. She wanted to trace a line of hungry kisses from his throat all the way down to the flatness of his belly whilst she watched his helpless reaction to her touch; she wanted to lace her fingers through the darkness of his body hair where it grew soft and thick around the base of his manhood; she wanted to slowly and thoroughly explore every rigid inch of that male part of him until she knew the shape, texture, heat, scent and taste of 'the pleasure giver—the great scimitar of love', as she had smiled to see it described in a book on the Middle East. Presumably the words sounded far more impressive in Arabic.

But she didn't need words—the image she had conjured up inside her head was enough to melt her bones—and the walls she had thrown up inside herself against this kind of desire. She should not have agreed to come here with him. She was too vulnerable, both to him and to the way she felt about him.

The way she loved him. The way she would always and for ever love only him. Fear quickened inside her, making her want to push back from the reality she had just exposed.

As a child, confronted with her parents' divorce, she had carefully picked up all the bits of the person who had once been her and tidied them away—just as her mother had always insisted she should pick up her toys and put them away. It had been her coping strategy then, and it still was now.

Only this time it wasn't working, and she wasn't coping—because this time her sexuality, which she had always so tightly controlled, had rebelled and broken down the doors to its prison. And, what was more, it had freed the emotion which had been its cellmate as well. Between the two of them they were now intent on taking over the controls.

This was crazy. How could she have let herself fall in love with Tariq?

Tariq looked down to where Gwynneth's hand lay against his arm.

No one—not anyone at all, not even when he had been a child—had managed to break through his barriers and touch the heart of his pain so immediately or so accurately.

But then, she was not just anyone. She was…

She was a woman with a string of lovers in her past, who could walk out of his life even more easily than his father had done and hurt him far more badly.

He lifted his own hand to remove hers from his body, but instead found he had placed it over hers, as though he wanted to keep it there.

How could a mere silence be this intense and profound? This charged with emotional and sensual urgency and promise? They were even breathing together, their hearts pumping the blood through their bodies in perfect time with one another. They stepped closer to one another, as though they were engaged in the mutually known steps of some intimate private dance. From one synchronised breath to the wild, driving thrust of his body and the clamouring, seeking need of her own to be filled with it—it was the dance of life itself, Gwynneth recognised.

Panic filled her. She wasn't ready for this; she was too afraid of the emotional pain that would follow. She snatched her hand away from under Tariq's and reminded him huskily, 'The women's quarters?'

'They're this way,' Tariq answered tersely, turning away

from her to stride so quickly down the corridor that she almost had to run to catch up with him.

When he eventually pushed open the fretted double doors at the end of the corridor, Gwynneth waited until she was sure she wasn't going to risk coming into any kind of contact with his body before she followed him into the room beyond them.

Large and rectangular, the room was decorated in a very Moorish style, with stylised arches and alcoves and fretwork. It was furnished with low divans piled high with richly coloured silk cushions and beautiful Persian rugs.

'This is the main salon. When the shutters are opened you will see that the room opens out onto a private courtyard. There are several bedrooms, all of which are prepared for occupation, so you may choose whichever you wish.'

'Which was your mother's?' Gwynneth asked. 'Only I wouldn't want to…'

'She had her own private suite within the women's quarters. It is closed up now. I suggest you use the room closest to this salon. It too has direct access to the garden.' He paused, the terseness leaving his voice as he added, 'I am afraid that until my staff return we shall be eating from the freezer. For myself I don't mind, but…'

'You can cook?' Gwynneth couldn't conceal her disbelief.

He gave a brief shrug. 'Of course—if I have to. I learned around the campfires of our people. But since there are only the two of us here it makes more sense to eat the meals my chef has prepared and frozen. I'll leave you to settle in now.'

Settle in? How could she do that when she was going to be living under the same roof with him? Get a grip, Gwynneth advised herself unkindly. You've been sharing a two-bedroomed apartment, now you're sharing a small palace. You probably won't even see him.

But somehow being here in what was the childhood home he had shared with his parents was far more intimate than sharing the apartment with him.

Although she had told herself she would not do so, in the end Gwynneth settled on the bedroom Tariq had suggested— because it had access to the courtyard garden with which she had fallen totally in love.

Tiled pathways led to rose-covered arbours, and beyond them to formal beds set out with plants and fruit trees. Fat goldfish swam lazily beneath the equally fat lily pads of the central pond. Beautifully detailed ornamental trellises divided the garden into separate rooms, each shaped like a pomegranate seed, which together, Gwynneth realized, formed a stylised pattern.

But surely best of all was what she thought must be an Arabian Nights version of the modern Western outdoor hot tub. Enclosed by gold-and-blue painted trelliswork and smothered in scented pink roses, the rich blue-tiled tub was semi-sunken into the ground. Opposite the tub was an alcove containing a low wide divan the size of a double bed, its rich blue cover heaped with crimson, gold and jade silk cushions, and on the table between the divan and the tub there were several glass perfume bottles.

The small area was a sybarite's paradise, and it was all too easy for Gwynneth to imagine some naked houri enjoying the scented warmth of the water whilst her robed lover reclined against the cushions, enjoying watching her. Perhaps he would go to her, feed her a piece of sugar-dusted Turkish delight from his own plate with one hand whilst with the other he slowly caressed the naked curves of her exposed breasts, tasted the damask darkness of her nipples…

Stop that, Gwynneth warned herself, as she wiggled her fingers experimentally in the crystal-clear water, savouring its warmth.

She really shouldn't be doing this, she told herself less than half an hour later, and she glanced round just to check that she was totally alone, before dropping the towel she had wrapped around herself and stepping into the tub. But she just hadn't been able to resist.

She reached for an overhanging rose that was already dropping its petals, harvesting them to scatter on the surface of the tub, breathing in their perfume.

The water closed round her body like warm silk. There was no real reason why she shouldn't indulge herself other than her own awareness of the sensuality of her private thoughts. But only she was privy to those, and, since Tariq had already said that he had work to do, she wasn't going to be disturbed.

Not by his presence, at least. But the thoughts she was having about him were certainly disturbing her, she admitted as she pushed through the water to the far side of the tub. A giveaway burn of colour heated her face as she felt the soft pressure of the water stroking between her legs as she moved. If she closed her eyes she could almost imagine that Tariq…

The unfamiliar sensuality of her thoughts might be making her face burn, but her self-consciousness wasn't strong enough to stop her hand from sliding down her body. Her breasts felt heavy, her nipples tight and aching. She was acutely physically aware of her own female flesh, of its pulse within the folds of her sex. She moved, not sure if her movement was designed to stop the quickening sensual beat or to savour it. She closed her eyes and let her body dictate to her mind the fantasy it wanted it to create. *Tariq.* His name filled the air around her, its vibration shimmering on the water and filling all her senses, even though she had only spoken it within herself.

Tariq pushed back his computer chair and stood up. He had just received an e-mail from the Chief of Police, informing him that he now believed they had all the potential danger and those responsible for it under control.

> I would ask that you remain in Mjenat for the time being, though. Until I am able to formally confirm that it is safe for you to return to Zuran City.

The Chief of Police and his men had been praiseworthily efficient and speedy. He glanced at his watch. He would go and tell Gwynneth. She would, he knew, be delighted to learn that their stay here in the villa was going to be so short-lived. And so, of course, was he.

So why did the prospect fill his heart with something more akin to heaviness than relief? He was falling victim to his own imaginings, he derided himself as he made his way towards the women's quarters.

The sitting room was empty, and then Tariq saw that the doors were open to the garden. He headed for them, stepping through them and out onto the tiled terrace. The garden was silent, apart from the singing of the birds, and then he heard the small sound of the movement of gently lapping water. He stepped out into the garden and stood there bareheaded, his concentration that of a desert hunter, watchful and still, before he started to walk, as soft-footed as a sleek-pelted panther, following the sound of the water.

She was half reclining, half seated in the hot tub, lying back, her eyes closed, her hair tied up on top of her head, loose tendrils caressing the pale oval of her face. Rose petals floated on the surface of the water, dappling small shadows through the water onto her naked body, their perfume intensified by the enclosed space and the heat of the sun. Unaware of his presence, she moved lazily in the water, her movement disturbing the petals and revealing the neat almost heart shape of her body hair, sleekly dark against the pearl beauty of her skin.

From where he was standing he could look down and see the delicate shaping of the outer lips of her sex, now furled as neatly and tightly together as the shell of an oyster. But, unlike the hard sharpness of a shell, the warm flesh of her lips could be teased apart by the stroke of his fingertip moving over and over again against them, until they swelled and parted of their own accord to offer him the pearl that lay within them, small and perfect, its female rigidity waiting eagerly for the caress of his hand and mouth.

The ache in his body pounded out its unmistakable message.

As he watched her she sighed and smiled, and lifted her hand to her midriff, letting it lie there as her fingers played against her own flesh. What was she thinking behind those closed eyelids? His own drooped as he let himself soak up the erotic visual stimulation of looking at her. A drifting rose petal rocked against the hard point of one not quite submerged nipple. A small convulsion rippled through her, as though even such slight stimulation was more than her body could endure without reacting. If a rose petal could do that, how would she react when it was his mouth that was stimulating those tight rose damson studs?

Swiftly and silently, without taking his gaze from her, he shed his clothes, the movement of his body as he stepped forward and leaned over her casting a shadow that flickered across her closed eyes.

By the time she had opened them he was already reaching into the water.

CHAPTER THIRTEEN

'TARIQ.'

Gwynneth stared up at him wonderingly. She had been daydreaming about him being here with her, and now he was. She exhaled on a long, slow sigh of arousal-induced acceptance.

'Shh.'

He reached into the water, one long finger slowly and delicately probing the soft closed lips of her sex whilst he watched her reaction darken her eyes and bring a sound of liquid pleasure to her lips. Her legs opened with the same sensual readiness as her sex. She felt warm and wet, his fingertip sliding slickly over the hard nub it was seeking. Tiny ripples scorched the surface of the water as she moved against his caress.

'No…' she protested helplessly, but her hands had already locked round his arm and her spine was arching up, bringing her breasts out of the water.

Tariq virtually felt his self-control shatter under the intensity of his response to her arousal. He released her briefly, a fine tremor jerking visibly through his body as he stepped into the tub to join her, his hands shaping her flesh beneath and above the water with a need he couldn't contain as he kneeled between her splayed legs. He kissed the taut arch of her throat and then her mouth, losing himself in its hot sweetness as he kissed her over and over again. The weight of her breasts filled his hands, his thumbs savouring the texture of her nipples as he rubbed his thumb-pads against their hardness.

'This is heaven,' Gwynneth whispered dreamily against his mouth. Her eyes shimmered with pleasure as she slid her fingers into the thick darkness of his hair, exploring the shape of his head, holding him against her so that she could taste and shape his lips with her tongue-tip before she plundered his mouth.

'I was lying here thinking about you, and now here you are...' she marvelled softly, knowing that what was happening was merely a dream. How could it possibly be anything else? How could Tariq be here with her, doing these incredibly sensual things to her and for her, otherwise? Because it was only happening inside her head she was free to enjoy it, free to say and do whatever she wished.

'Your thoughts must have called me to you,' Tariq told her softly, cupping her face between his hands, stroking his fingers slowly along the sensitive curve behind her earlobes.

She lifted her hands to his shoulders. His flesh felt warm and supple as her fingertips trailed over the muscles beneath his skin. His hands moved down her back and then round to cup her breasts, whilst he laced kisses along her jaw and down her neck.

Gwynneth trembled, letting her pleasure take hold of her and fill her.

His thumb-pads slowly circled the dark arousal-flushed aureoles, ignoring the fierce demand of her erect nipples. Only the lower half of her body was still beneath the water now, and Tariq was slowly kissing his way down to the valley between her breasts. And then up the slope of one of them, his tongue-tip following the circle being traced by his thumb, and then moving closer and closer to her nipple.

She trembled and moaned softly, and as though she had given a specific instruction his hand slipped between her still open legs, his fingers quickly finding the pulsing pearl within the oyster of her sex and plucking rhythmically at it. She could feel his tongue stroking against her nipple in time to the caress of his fingers, drawing from her such an intense reaction that her whole body was seized with her convulsive response to it. It gripped her, not gently but fiercely, almost frighteningly, so that she tensed against its possession, fearing its power over her.

'Relax.' Tariq whispered the word against her breast before his lips closed over her nipple and his fingers slid the length of her sex and began oh so slowly and carefully to penetrate its wetness.

She couldn't bear the pleasure of what he was doing to her. It was taking her and possessing her and rendering her helpless as it gripped and savaged her.

This was no dream.

'I think,' she heard Tariq murmur, lifting his mouth from her breast to her lips and from there making a deliciously slow and thorough journey to her ear, 'that this is something I would prefer to accomplish at leisure and on dry land.'

Gwynneth nodded her head.

'Hold on, then,' he told her, scooping her up and starting to carry her to the edge of the tub.

Her arms wrapped tightly around his neck and her head resting on his chest, Gwynneth looked down the length of his body, her breath leaving her lungs on an unsteady exhalation. He was big, but then she already knew that from that first night. And he was very aroused. As he stepped down onto the tiles she removed one arm from his neck, unable to stop herself from reaching out to circle the engorged head of his sex with one uncertain speculative fingertip before stroking the full length of him and back again.

The awareness came to her out of nowhere that she was changed for ever now, and there was no going back. Her body, her senses, would remember this pleasure for ever, and her own helpless captivity by it. A fierce pang of need tightened her body and then released it into a series of small quivering shudders.

'You've caught the sun on your shoulders,' Tariq told her. 'Does it hurt?'

'All I can feel is how much I want you,' Gwynneth admitted boldly, as he carried her over to the daybed and placed her on it. 'I've fought against feeling like this all my life,' she whispered emotionally, 'and now I know why. It *is* every bit as dangerous as I was always afraid it would be. More so, in fact.' She gave a small shudder, her eyes dark and huge as she asked huskily, 'If I feel like this now, how will I feel when you're deep inside me?'

Exhaling jaggedly, she reached up to stroke her fingertips along his forearm as he leaned over her and brushed the hair off her face.

'Much the same as you felt with your other lovers, I imagine,' he told her lightly.

Watching the stillness invade her body was like watching the sunlight fade from the desert, leaving it cold and barren. He stared at her, waiting for her to explain her reaction.

'Actually, there haven't been any others,' Gwynneth told him carefully.

She could feel him looking at her, willing her to look back at him, but she felt too self-conscious to be able to do so. He was bound to be shocked to learn that she had never had full sex—what man would not be?

When the seconds ticking by without him saying anything became totally unbearable, she forced herself to whisper croakily, 'I suppose you're turned off, now aren't you?'

'Yes,' he said curtly. 'Totally turned off. Any man worthy of the name would be—just as no woman who values what she is would ever think that she was flattering a man by assuming that he wanted her to pretend to be a youthful innocent. I don't merely find it a turn-off to be classed as the type of adult male who is excited by the thought of having sex with a virgin, I also find it offensive,' he said pithily. 'I'm a fully adult man. I don't need or require a fully adult woman to pretend for my benefit that she's a virgin.'

Gwynneth could hear the savage distaste in his voice. 'But I'm not—' She began to defend herself, and then stopped.

'No, neither am I anymore,' Tariq agreed. He had placed her discarded towel across his body, so that it was impossible for her to see whether he was still aroused or not—not that she had any intention of challenging him. The very thought threatened to cripple her emotionally and sexually.

Instead she gave a small, proud shrug and told him defensively, 'You were the one who came on to me.'

He looked at her in silence for so long that her heart began to beat in uncoordinated jerky thuds of apprehension.

'Correction. I took what you were offering. A woman does not bathe naked, exhibiting herself as you were, in the proximity of a man if she does not want him to be aware of her.'

There was nothing she could say to that, no defence she could honestly make, and her face stung with the heat of her humiliation and anger.

Whilst he had been speaking she had resorted to tucking several cushions strategically around herself, to screen her body, and now, as he stood up, she deliberately looked away from him so that he couldn't accuse her of anything else.

'I came to see what time you wanted to eat. Here in Zuran we eat later in the evening than you might in Britain, to benefit from the coolness.'

'I'm not really hungry.' Her voice sounded as brittle as her pride felt. She could hear the rustle of fabric and guessed that he was dressing.

'We'll eat later, then,' he told her blandly.

Tariq stood facing into the light breeze that was coming off the oasis, enjoying its freshness. In the reeds a bird called warningly to its mate, and in the moonlight he could see a fish jumping to snap at a hovering gnat.

Beneath his robe his body ached with unsatisfied desire. It was a dull heavy pulse he couldn't ignore, threatening to flare into almost priapic fury with every breath he took. Not even the sharp, destructive thrust of disappointment followed by distaste he had felt for Gwynneth's unwholesome claim to innocence had the power to silence the sexual clamour of his body. Her play-acting had destroyed something that for him had been uniquely rare. He had thought from the conversations they had shared that she would be above that sort of thing, that they were beginning to share something very special and that she would be honest with him instead of lying to him.

He remembered that he hadn't told her that they would soon be free to leave. Why not? There was no purpose in them staying here—no purpose in him hoping that they could share more than merely a relationship based on the sexual hunger they felt for one another.

And he had wanted that? Now who was playing games? he taunted himself. Of course he'd wanted that, and he'd wanted much more. He'd wanted… He'd wanted *her*, in his bed and in his life. He'd wanted her to give herself to him fully and completely, heart and soul, with honesty and commitment and love, and instead she had offered him a puerile claim to fake virginity.

As soon as they had eaten he would tell her that they were going back to Zuran.

Her shoulders, her back and her upper arms all stung slightly with the pain of her sunburned skin, and Gwynneth winced as she saw the bright red glow of it in the mirror. It wasn't bad enough to warrant being described as true sunburn, but it still tingled uncomfortably. She had been a fool to give in to the temptation of using the hot tub—and not just because of her sunburn.

The last thing she felt like doing was having to face Tariq again, but she had a feeling that if she didn't turn up then he would come looking for her, and if he found her in bed, using the excuse of her sore skin so as not to have to eat with him, he was all too likely to imagine that she was trying to seduce him, she decided bitterly.

Tariq had said that they might as well eat in his private quarters, which were on the opposite side of the villa. It was nearly ten o'clock—the time at which he had suggested they should eat. It was a pity she hadn't brought something with her that she could drape round her shoulders, she acknowledged, as she pulled a small face at her own reflection. Bright pink skin and a matt black strappy top. What a combination. But she didn't have any other choice.

Tariq was waiting for her in the entrance hall, the cold reserve of his voice as he said, 'I was just about to come and find you,' making her feel glad that he hadn't needed to do so.

The room he escorted her to was surprisingly modern, given the traditional style of the villa, and somehow the combination of the traditional design of the room teamed with pared-down modern furniture was one that soothed and yet also tantalised the senses. The sleek lines of the ebony console and coffee tables paired with off-white leather sofas over which brilliantly coloured kilims had been carelessly but effectively thrown created a room that offered comfort and style, its starkness broken by the splashes of rich colour. Paintings and sculptures echoed the brilliant flashes of colour, making Gwynneth itch to reach out and touch a painting thick with crimson and orange paint, depicting the sun rising over the rawness of the desert.

Double doors opened into a smaller dining room with a wall of huge glass doors, beyond which lay an illuminated courtyard.

'I have my own small kitchen on the other side of the dining room,' Tariq explained. 'Sometimes it is simpler and easier to cater for myself, and when I had these rooms converted for my own use I included a small kitchen so that I didn't have to invade Arub's territory and provoke an outcry.'

'Is there anything I can do to help?' Gwynneth asked him, feeling awkward.

'No. Everything's ready.'

She could see that he was frowning as he looked at her.

'Your skin looks sore,' he commented.

'It looks worse than it is,' Gwynneth assured him lightly.

'And it's my own fault. I should have taken more care.' And not just against the danger of the sun. She had no idea how it was possible to love a man so much whilst knowing that doing so was self-damaging. But she did know that she wasn't the first woman to discover that it was. The best possible thing for her would be to return to Britain and forget that she had ever met Tariq. Even supposing he had made love to her, it would not have meant anything. Having sex with a man you loved but who did not love you must surely be one of the most soul-destroying things a woman could experience. Unless she managed to temporarily deceive herself that he *did* love her—if she could do that she could always carry with her a very special memory. But the memory would be a lie.

Only if she let it be, a dangerous inner voice whispered.

Determinedly squashing it into silence, she took a deep breath and asked Tariq, 'How long do you think we will have to stay here?'

He looked away from her, as though something else had caught his attention, his voice slightly blurred as he told her dismissively, 'It's impossible to say.'

He was deliberately lying to her, Tariq knew. He, a man who prided himself on his honesty. Why lie to keep her here after the angry revulsion he had felt earlier? Because that angry revulsion had been caused by his feelings for her. He had felt let down by her, disappointed in her after the emotional intensity created when they had talked. Then she had somehow reached out to him, touched all the sore places within him and soothed them as no other person ever had, and because of that he had let down his guard and allowed himself to admit that his feelings for her went much deeper than merely sexual desire.

Holding her in his arms as he'd carried her to the daybed earlier, he had not checked the words of love and adoration forming inside his head, waiting to spill from his lips and be whispered against her skin. He had, he had thought then, formed a bond, adult to adult—a bedrock on which they could build a love that would sustain them for ever.

His tutors had warned him as a young man that he was too idealistic and that his ideals would be a heavy burden for others to carry.

They ate in a silence broken only by Gwynneth's slightly stilted complimentary comments about their food.

'My chef knows that I prefer to eat naturally produced food simply prepared, so that its flavours aren't obscured,' Tariq informed her, before suggesting, 'If you've finished eating, I suggest a stroll through the gardens to aid the digestion.'

'It sounds a good idea.' Gwynneth agreed. 'But please don't let me disrupt your normal routine. There's no need for you to accompany me.'

Something about his narrow-eyed gaze made her skin prickle uncomfortably.

'As you wish,' he agreed. 'Do you have some lotion for your skin?'

'No, I haven't,' Gwynneth admitted. 'But, as I said, it looks worse than it feels.'

'Maybe so, but it would still be wise to soothe it,' Tariq told her, commanding brusquely, 'Come with me.'

His hand was on her arm and it was all she could do not to tense betrayingly—but the sensitivity of her flesh had nothing to do with the sun and everything to do with Tariq himself. It was his touch that was affecting her so intensely and so intimately that she could hardly bear even to stand close to him, never mind be touched by him as he guided her out of the room and down an unfamiliar corridor.

It was only when he had opened the door and almost thrust her inside that she realised the room he had taken her to was his own bedroom. Like the other rooms, this one was a skilful blend of traditional and modern, its walls painted a flat shade of off-white to heighten the richness of the fabrics that that been used. Deep jewel shades in heavy silk fabric covered the chairs and the low divan, as well as the huge bed, echoing the colours in the rugs scattered on the polished wooden floor and hanging on the walls, whilst plain, fine white muslin curtains hung at the windows, caught back in intricately designed metal clasps.

'Wait here,' Tariq instructed, going to open a door which she could see led into a very modern crisp matt white and chrome bathroom.

The room held a very faint but altogether disturbing tang of the cool, discreet cologne Tariq wore, and Gwynneth had to catch herself up to stop herself from closing her eyes, the better to breathe in and relish the intimacy of it.

Tariq reappeared from the bathroom holding a plastic bottle of soothing skin lotion.

'I like to keep a reasonably well-stocked medicine cabinet here. Sometimes the young volunteers who come out to work with the archaeologists forget how dangerous the sun can be, even in the winter.'

Gwynneth smiled her polite thanks as she reached out to take the lotion from him. But instead of giving it to her he walked over to the bed and threw back the heavy cover to reveal the immaculate white bedlinen underneath it.

Gwynneth stared at the bed as though she had never seen one

before. Her heart was pounding ridiculously heavily, all her senses so acutely alive that her awareness of him unnerved her.

'I imagine that your back has suffered the most damage,' he told her coolly. 'If you want to sit on the bed, I'll put some of this on for you.'

CHAPTER FOURTEEN

SHE could have given any number of responses to that. But what with her emotions screaming a panicky *No, no, no and no again*, and the effort it took to keep the words inside her head instead of allowing them to her lips, all she could manage was a red-faced stutter. 'I…I can do it myself.'

One dark eyebrow rose in a mixture of disbelief and impatience.

'I doubt it.'

'Truthfully, I think I can manage to do it myself—and it isn't really hurting.'

Her face was as pink as her bare arms and she looked as modestly apprehensive as though they were strangers, and she was the kind of woman who was reluctant to expose her body even to the gaze of a lover. And, what was more, she wasn't faking her self-consciousness, Tariq recognised.

He dismissed this somewhat contradictory realisation with a mental shrug. He had no idea what exactly it was that was causing her apprehension, but she was perfectly safe from any threat from him.

'Despite your denials, I refuse to believe that you aren't in some discomfort,' he informed her dryly.

Oh, she was. But it was not the kind of discomfort he meant! Hers sprang from her awareness of what was going to happen to her the minute he touched her, and it had nothing to do with a bit of sunburn.

It was panic that was making her body tremble slightly as she turned her back, wasn't it? Certainly not excitement.

'This would be easier without your top,' Tariq pointed out.

'What? No!' Before she could stop herself Gwynneth had turned round, her face burning far more hotly than her body as she tried to control her own thoughts. And desires. Because she did desire him, didn't she? Her breath came quickly, in soft short bursts, as she struggled against the knowledge of just how much she loved him.

'You were naked in the pool, and therefore the whole of your back will have caught the sun,' he was saying, almost prosaically.

Why was she dragging out this torment? He was obviously determined to administer the lotion, and very probably capable of removing her top himself if she didn't do so for him. She might as well let him go ahead and get it over with as quickly as possible, Gwynneth told herself miserably, exhaling as she turned her back on him and tugged off her top.

Still keeping her back to him, she perched on the corner of the bed. She could feel the warmth of Tariq's breath against the nape of her neck, and then the firmness of his lotion-cooled hands. She gasped as she felt the coldness of the lotion on her sun-warmed flesh, and then suppressed a far more betraying gasp as Tariq started to smooth it into her skin, stroking and massaging his way up her spine, smoothing it round her ribcage so that his fingertips brushed against her breasts. Then, whilst her nipples were still peaking in arousal, making her stiffen every muscle apprehensively as she tried to control her need, he moved up to her shoulders, where he paused to push her hair out of the way before massaging the lotion into the back of her neck.

'Thank you—' she began, desperate to escape before she totally disgraced herself and let him see how much she wanted him. But she couldn't pull away because his hands were still resting on her shoulders.

'It was my pleasure.'

Was something wrong with her hearing? And, if not, why did his voice sound so thick and filled with pain?

'My pleasure,' he repeated. 'And my torment.'

Now she couldn't stop herself from turning to look at him.

'Tariq—' she began, and then stopped when Tariq leaned towards her, covering her mouth with his and kissing her with the kind of passion she had been yearning for.

Eagerly she kissed him back, parting her lips to the possessive demand of his tongue, clinging to his shoulders as he picked her up bodily and placed her on the bed.

'No words,' he told her as he joined her there. 'Not anything but this, my Gwynneth. Just this and us…'

Just us! Gwynneth closed her eyes and gave herself up to the magical touch of his hands, sighing in wanton pleasure as she felt them sliding over her. She wriggled out of her skirt and watched his eyes darken as he studied her almost naked body.

'Lie down.'

Quivering with excitement, she did so, watching him as he reached for the bottle of lotion.

There was no sunburn where he was using the pads of his thumbs to massage deliberately sensual slow circles of delicious pleasure, on the flesh just above the curve of her buttocks. But she didn't care. All she cared about was that he kept on doing what he was doing and didn't stop. How was it possible with such a simple touch for him to make her body respond to him in the way it was doing right now? She wanted to stretch out beneath those massaging fingers. She wanted to sigh and moan, to arch her spine and open her legs, to…

She felt him removing the tiny fluted-leg briefs that hugged her hips, barely covering her bottom.

'Oh, yes…' Had she actually said that or, please heaven, merely thought it? she wondered hazily as Tariq stroked the lotion into the round globes of her buttocks and then down the backs of her thighs.

'Turn over.' The words were a command, but his hoarse tones made them sound almost like a plea.

Gwynneth gave a voluptuous sigh and turned over, looking up at him, her flesh and her senses flooded with the sensuality he had aroused. Her whole body felt boneless and soft, his to mould and caress as he wished. The same bonelessness seemed to have softened the resistance from her thoughts as well, turned her into a creature of willing compliance…

She held her breath she watched as him undress, her expression mirroring everything that she was feeling. Had he ever seen a woman look at him like this before? Tariq wondered. If he had he couldn't remember it. Gwynneth's gaze, so openly aroused and ardent as it looked and lingered where he was already erect and ready for her, and her tongue-tip moistening her lips was the most powerful aphrodisiac he had ever known. Without speaking to him, without touching him, without him touching her, she had told him how it was going to be. How she would hold him within the warm caress of her body whilst he plunged within it over and over again, until he took them both over the edge of that cliff at the end of the universe beyond which lay eternity itself.

The way Tariq was looking at her made words redundant, Gwynneth knew. A thousand times a thousand words would not be enough to convey all that he was conveying to her as their gazes meshed, hers clinging desperately to his, knowing he was telling her that he was taking her into a place so far away from anything she knew that, once there, she would be wholly dependent on him.

When he came down to her, the feel of his skin on hers was like the cool brush of silk, and the weight of his body answered a need she had not previously known she had. When he kissed her mouth it was slowly and lingeringly, savouring the taste and texture of her as she lay supine and soft beneath him, letting him take her where he wanted to go.

He kissed her again, more deeply, causing her body to arch up off the bed to his. Gwynneth clung to him, too afraid of what was happening to her to risk letting go and being left alone in the maelstrom of her own desire.

He kissed her throat and behind her ear, and then the curve of her shoulder, and her fingers curled into his flesh whilst her nipples pushed up against him.

When he kissed the slope of her breast her fingers splayed against his buttocks, holding him tight against her body. She was on fire for him now, consumed by a throbbing, pounding ache that beat through her in hot demand.

His tongue flicked against her nipple, making her shudder in the spasm of erotic delight that gripped her. When he raked her nipple gently with his teeth she cried out against the pleasure, welcoming the weight of his hand cupping her sex and momentarily soothing its need. She was open and ready for his touch, the swollen lips flushed with desire and as juicily ripe as the sweetest peach.

Tariq could feel the ache in his own body to taste and enjoy her. He kissed his way down her belly, his heart pounding heavily with the weight of his need as he rubbed the tip of his tongue over the pulsing thrust of her clitoris, feeling it swell and harden within his caress. Her soft cries of shocked pleasure drove him on to take her further and deeper, until her arousal overwhelmed her.

Gwynneth tried to hold back what she was feeling, what she was being driven to feel by the caress of Tariq's tongue, but it was impossible It crashed down over her and through her in surge upon surge of molten liquid pleasure until it finally receded, leaving her behind, satisfied and yet somehow not satisfied, fulfilled and yet still craving some other deeper unknown pleasure—a craving she had to communicate to him.

'Tariq, I want you.' Had she said it or only felt it? Was Tariq responding to her words or his own need when he held her and kissed her, with the taste of her own self still on his lips? Over and over again, his tongue thrust deeper and deeper within the warm cavity of her mouth, whilst his hands slid to her hips to lift and ready her.

It didn't matter how many men there had been, just so long as from this moment forward there was only him, Tariq thought passionately, all his doubts and reservations washed away by the overpowering surge of his love for her. Clean and new and whole, it filled and humbled him. She was so incomparably precious to him. She made him feel a thousand and one things he had never known it was possible to feel, and in a thousand and one different and unique ways. She touched the deepest part of him and brought it and him to life. Who could understand love? A man could merely experience it, give himself up to it and to the woman for whom he was born.

I love you. The words filled his head and his heart as he took Gwynneth's mouth in a kiss of possession and commitment, releasing his body to sink deep into her sleekly muscled warmth, and then deeper still. Only he couldn't. And she was lying rigidly beneath him, her eyes open wide with shocked apprehension and pain.

Whilst his mind grappled with the true meaning of her body's tightly held muscles, his body gave in to its own driving need. One thrust, fierce and quick, made her cry out, and then she was clinging to him, her eyes shimmering with the same emotion he could feel glittering in his own.

Gwynneth could feel Tariq's shock, but already the brief sharp pain was fading, to be replaced by a pulsing ache to feel him deeper inside her.

'No,' she whispered possessively as he tried to pull back. 'No…' As though to demonstrate her determination she moved against him, holding his gaze with her own until he gave in, shuddering with the release of his own tension. Slowly and carefully he thrust into her again, deeper and then deeper still, as she clung demandingly to him, grinding her hips against his, until he moved faster and deeper and her own body picked up the rhythm of his and moved in counterpoint to it. Up and up he took her, until there was nowhere left to go, and then they were poised on the pinnacle of a pleasure so acute it made her cry out in sweet agony as it pierced her. She felt its fierce surge grip her in the same heartbeat as Tariq gave a guttural moan of release and she felt the heat of his completion pulsing inside her.

* * *

'I've brought you a cup of tea.'

No matter how hard she tried, Gwynneth could neither control the hot colour storming her face, nor bring herself to look directly at Tariq as he put the tea on the bedside table next to her and then sat down on the bed.

'Is there any news yet about when—when we can leave here?' she asked unevenly. The last thing she wanted was for him to fear she was going to use what had happened last night as a means to try to cling to him. She had more pride than that!

She wanted to leave? After what they had shared? Tariq felt his heart slalom inside his chest wall. Too late to stop the pain wrenching him apart. No way was he letting her leave. Not now and, if he had his way, not ever. And certainly not before he had an opportunity to find a way to convince her that she wanted to spend the rest of her life with him as passionately as he wanted to spend his with her.

'No, not as yet,' he lied.

'Oh.' Gwynneth tried discreetly to moisten her dry lips with the tip of her tongue. She couldn't believe she had actually slept so deeply that she hadn't even known that Tariq was sleeping next to her. But it was obvious from the dent in the pillow and the scent of him all around her that he had done. It was too late now for her to grieve for the memories she might have stored up.

'I owe you an apology,' Tariq announced tersely.

Gwynneth plucked nervously at the sheet.

'I can understand why you would think… I mean why you wouldn't have thought…' She wrinkled her nose and took a deep breath. 'It is unusual for a woman of my age to be… I mean, not to have…'

'So why?' Tariq asked her.

'My father,' Gwynneth answered him honestly. 'As I told you, he was something of a sexual predator—a man who believed that sex was an appetite to be enjoyed and who didn't see why it should have any connection with his emotions. After he left, my mother used to complain that I was like him. I think that was one of the reasons she didn't want to have me around.'

Tariq looked away from her. There wasn't even the vaguest hint of self-pity in her voice, but he knew if he looked at her he wouldn't be able to stop himself from taking her in his arms and telling her exactly what he thought of both her parents, and especially her mother.

'I suppose it started then in a way,' Gwynneth admitted. 'Although I was too young to connect what I was feeling with sex. I just knew that I didn't want to be like my father. It was only when I got older, hearing him talk openly and without shame about his sex life, that I began to worry that I might have inherited whatever traits he possessed that were responsible for his immoral behaviour. Sex was just a physical appetite to him—the pursuit of a woman for sex was a challenge he couldn't resist. He loved the thrill of a new sexual conquest, but he was incapable of making any kind of real emotional contact with a partner. I was afraid that I might end up the same, so I decided that I wasn't going to have sex—and, more importantly, that I wasn't going to *want* to have sex. And it worked. I didn't. Until that first night with you. And then I realised…'

Abruptly Gwynneth stopped speaking, her face burning as she realised how close she had come to telling him that the knowledge that she had fallen in love with him had shown her how very different she was from her father.

'You realised what?' Tariq probed.

'I realised that I was missing out on a lot of fun, and that I didn't after all want to spend the rest of my life as a virgin,' she made herself say, as lightly as she could.

'Fun?'

'Well, I certainly enjoyed last night,' she told him.

Tariq looked at her. This wasn't what he wanted to hear.

What he wanted to hear was that in his arms she had realised that she couldn't live without him, that she loved him and she wanted to spend the rest of her life with him. And he was pretty sure that was *exactly* what she felt, having listened to her talking about her father and seen the shadows of her past lying darkly in her eyes.

He'd never been a gambler, but some things were so important that a man had to risk something of great value in order to gamble with life for the prize he wanted. Right now he was gambling with his pride. And Tariq's wasn't just any old male pride: it was the kind of pride it took generations of alpha male history to create.

'Really?' he asked her smoothly. 'How much?'

'H-how much?' Gwynneth wondered wildly what on earth she could say. This wasn't the way she had expected the conversation to proceed.

'Yes, how much? Enough, for instance, to do it again tonight?'

Gwynneth's heart was pounding so loudly she could hardly think.

'Er…yes. I mean, if you want to.'

'So, tonight, then?' he repeated, ignoring her small rider. 'And what about right now?'

'Right now?' A betraying ache was spreading through her body. 'Well…'

'Or maybe right now, tonight and all the nights for the rest of our lives?' Tariq suggested softly. 'And not because it was *fun*, but because we can't bear to be apart—because we love each other so much that life apart would be like the desert without the warmth of the sun or the water of its oases, an endless sterile darkness in which nothing could exist or survive. Because together we want to create the new life that will be our child, conceived and born in love—our love. Because we feel all those things for one another, and so much more I can't put into words. You have become my morning sunrise, Gwynneth, and my evening sunset. And all the hours of my life in between.'

'You…you *love* me?' Gwynneth felt as though all the blood had suddenly drained from her veins, leaving her hollow and light-headed.

'Can you doubt it? If you do, then at least allow me to spend the rest of our lives proving it to you—as my wife.'

'You want to *marry* me?' Gwynneth whispered, sitting bolt upright in the bed, oblivious to her nudity, the colour beating up under her skin. 'This is crazy. You're a prince. Princes marry princesses…'

Tariq was shaking his head. 'Not this prince. He marries only where he loves, and he loves you, only you and always you.'

The look in her eyes betrayed her, making Tariq hold his breath against the sudden fierce rush of exultation that seized him.

'Please don't,' Gwynneth begged him. 'Please don't look at me like that!'

'All right,' Tariq agreed easily. 'How about if I do this instead?'

She was so unprepared for him to take hold of her and kiss

her that she had no defence against the slow sweetness of her own helpless pleasure.

'I love you,' Tariq whispered against her lips. 'I wanted to tell you so last night, before I made you mine, but somehow the words never got spoken.'

'You loved me then…when you still thought…?'

'I fell in love with the woman you are, Gwynneth. With you, not your virginity,' he told her firmly. 'Now, please, put me out of my misery and tell me. Will you give me your love? Will you share my life and my hopes and ideals? Will you allow me to love and cherish and—?'

'Yes!' Gwynneth stopped him, the joy of what she was hearing filling her heart to the brim with happiness. To know that he loved her when she had believed he did not, when she had believed that her own once-in-a-lifetime love for him could never be returned, was a once-in-for-ever kind of very special happiness, she decided. She put her hand in his and then leaned forward to whisper lovingly against his mouth, 'Yes, yes, yes, yes, *yes*…' Until he silenced her with his kiss.

EPILOGUE

'HAPPY?' Tariq asked, his voice holding both tenderness and passion. 'No regrets?'

Gwynneth smiled up at him and shook her head. They were sharing the same rose-shaded and scented bathing pool where, in what now seemed like another life, she had lain alone in the sun-warmed water and indulged in what had then seemed like an impossible fantasy.

But, as she had now discovered, reality could sometimes be infinitely better than fantasy.

'How could I when I have you—and this?' she whispered softly, reaching up to kiss him with her newfound knowledge of just how sweetly vulnerable he was to her kisses.

'You love me?'

His voice was rougher now. Gwynneth nodded her head.

'Say it,' Tariq begged her hungrily. 'Let me hear the words.'

'I love you, Tariq,' she told him, laughing softly when he scarcely allowed her to finish before taking her in his arms and kissing her with a passion that set the rose petals that floated on the water surging rhythmically on small waves created by the eager movement of her body against his.

It had been her choice that they should honeymoon here

in the Hidden Valley, and although Tariq had insisted that she was free to choose any destination she wished, she had seen in his eyes how much her choice had touched his emotions.

'I want to come back every year of our lives together to celebrate our anniversary here,' Gwynneth told him lovingly, and then leaned forward to whisper in his ear, 'Do you realise that it's lunchtime and over three hours since breakfast?'

'You're hungry?'

'Yes—but for you, not food,' she told him boldly.

The colour came and went in her face, and, watching her, he wondered if even now, after he had told her so a hundred thousand times and more, she really knew just how much he loved her—just how complete his world was with her in it and how empty it would be without her.

'Here?' he suggested.

'In the pool?' Longing and excitement darkened the gaze she turned on him.

They had had so few opportunities for shared intimacy these last few weeks, in the run-up to the wedding, but now at last she had Tariq to herself.

When they returned to Zuran it would be to live in a rented villa until their own new villa was ready. Tariq was insistent that they had their own home, rather than live as part of his extended family, but she had told him that she wanted their villa to be close enough to the palace for him to be able to visit as often as he wished.

She was far from the first British bride to be welcomed into the Zurani royal family, and it had brought happy tears to her eyes to discover that the extended family members were so willing to become her friends.

She stroked his arm, still thinking of family. 'It was so

thoughtful of you to arrange for Teresa and baby Anthony to be flown out to our wedding.'

'They are a part of our family, and it was only right and proper that they should be there.'

His reply might sound formal and distant, but there was nothing distant about his generosity towards her half-brother and his mother. Not only had he taken on the financial responsibility for Anthony's education, he was also making Teresa an allowance that had enabled her to return home and set up her own small business.

Thinking of baby Anthony, and the gorgeous children of Tariq's extended family, caused a small fluttering sensation to tighten in her own body.

'It still scares me to think how close I came to listening to my fears instead of to my heart. In refusing to accept that I loved you I would have lost so much…'

'No. I would not have allowed that to happen—and besides, the fault was mine for so stupidly misjudging you,' he told her lovingly. 'Somehow I would have found a way to open the doors of your heart to my love, Gwynneth. I would never have given up—just as I will never give you up now. You are my love and my life, my heart, and all of me that goes beyond that. It is my belief that we were destined to be together, that we were created for one another, and that we fit together as one perfect whole in every single way.'

Emotional tears stung her eyes. She loved him so much, and to hear him voice his love for her had the power to touch the deepest wellspring of her feelings.

'I want our first child to be conceived here, Tariq,' she told him huskily. 'Here in this valley that is so much a part of your

heritage and where we first loved one another. Here and…
and now.'

She trembled as he lifted her bodily from the water and bent
to take her mouth in a fiercely passionate kiss, ready to begin.

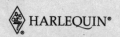

HARLEQUIN®

American ROMANCE®

IS PROUD TO PRESENT A GUEST APPEARANCE BY

QUILL
BOOK
AWARD
WINNING
AUTHOR

NEW YORK TIMES bestselling author
DEBBIE MACOMBER

The Wyoming Kid

The story of an ex–rodeo cowboy,
a schoolteacher and their journey to the altar.

**The Wyoming Kid is available from
Harlequin American Romance in July 2006.**